THE WEIRDSTONE OF BRISINGAMEN

THE WEIRDSTONE

OF BRISINGAMEN

A TALE OF ALDERLEY

Alan Garner

Henry Z. Walck, Inc.　　　New York

Garner, Alan
   The weirdstone of Brisingamen; a tale
of Alderley.   Walck, 1969
   253p.

   Goblins, witches, and warlocks are
after the magic stone which Susan wears
on her bracelet in this exciting story.

1. England - Fiction   2. Fantasy
I. Title

This edition for my parents

CONTENTS

THE WEIRDSTONE OF BRISINGAMEN

THE LEGEND OF ALDERLEY

In every prayer I offer up, Alderley,
and all belonging to it, will be ever a
living thought in my heart.
                    Rev. Edward Stanley: 1837

AT DAWN one still October day in the long ago of the world, across the hill of Alderley, a farmer from Mobberley was riding to Macclesfield fair.

The morning was dull, but mild; light mists bedimmed his way; the woods were hushed; the day promised fine. The farmer was in good spirits, and he let his horse, a milk-white mare, set her own pace, for he wanted her to arrive fresh for the market. A rich man would walk back to Mobberley that night.

So, his mind in the town while he was yet on the hill, the farmer drew near to the place known as Thieves' Hole. And there the horse stood still and would answer to neither spur nor rein. The spur and rein she understood, and her master's stern command, but the eyes that held her were stronger than all of these.

In the middle of the path, where surely there had been

no one, was an old man, tall, with long hair and beard. "You go to sell this mare," he said. "I come here to buy. What is your price?"

But the farmer wished to sell only at the market, where he would have the choice of many offers, so he rudely bade the stranger quit the path and let him through, for if he stayed longer he would be late to the fair.

"Then go your way," said the old man. "None will buy. And I shall await you here at sunset."

The next moment he was gone, and the farmer could not tell how or where.

The day was warm, and the tavern cool, and all who saw the mare agreed that she was a splendid animal, the pride of Cheshire, a queen among horses; and everyone said that there was no finer beast in the town. But no one offered to buy. A sour-eyed farmer rode out of Macclesfield at the end of the day.

Near Thieves' Hole the mare stopped: the stranger was there.

Thinking any price now better than none, the farmer agreed to sell. "How much will you give?" he said.

"Enough. Now come with me."

By Seven Firs and Goldenstone they went, to Stormy Point and Saddlebole. And they halted before a great rock embedded in the hillside. The old man lifted his staff and lightly touched the rock, and it split with the noise of thunder.

2

At this, the farmer toppled from his plunging horse and, on his knees, begged the other to have mercy on him and let him go his way unharmed. The horse should stay; he did not want her. Only spare his life, that was enough.

The wizard, for such he was, commanded the farmer to rise. "I promise you safe conduct," he said. "Do not be afraid; for living wonders you shall see here."

Beyond the rock stood a pair of iron gates. These the wizard opened, and took the farmer and his horse down a narrow tunnel deep into the hill. A light, subdued but beautiful, marked their way. The passage ended, and they stepped into a cave, and there a wondrous sight met the farmer's eyes—a hundred and forty knights in silver armor, and by the side of all but one a milk-white mare.

"Here they lie in enchanted sleep," said the wizard, "until a day will come—and come it will—when England shall be in direst peril, and England's mothers weep. Then out from the hill these must ride and, in a battle thrice lost, thrice won, upon the plain, drive the enemy into the sea."

The farmer, dumb with awe, turned with the wizard into a further cavern, and here mounds of gold and silver and precious stones lay strewn along the ground.

"Take what you can carry in payment for the horse."

And when the farmer had crammed his pockets (ample as his lands!), his shirt, and his fists with jewels, the wizard hurried him up the long tunnel and thrust him out of the gates. The farmer stumbled, the thunder rolled, he looked,

3

and there was only the rock above him. He was alone on the hill, near Stormy Point. The broad full moon was up, and it was night.

And although in later years he tried to find the place, neither he nor any after him ever saw the iron gates again. Nell Beck swore she saw them once, but she was said to be mad, and when she died they buried her under a hollow bank near Brindlow wood in the field that bears her name to this day.

PART 1

1

HIGHMOST REDMANHEY

THE GUARD knocked on the door of the compartment as he went past. "Wilmslow fifteen minutes!"

"Thank you!" shouted Colin.

Susan began to clear away the debris of the journey—apple cores, orange peel, food wrappings, magazines, while Colin pulled down their luggage from the rack. And within three minutes they were both poised on the edge of their seats, case in hand and raincoat over one arm, caught, like every traveler before or since, in that limbo of journey's end, when there is nothing to do and no time to relax. Those last miles were the longest of all.

The platform of Wilmslow station was thick with people, and more spilled off the train, but Colin and Susan had no difficulty in recognizing Gowther Mossock among those waiting. As the tide of passengers broke around him and surged through the gates, leaving the children lonely at the far end of the platform, he waved his hand and came striding toward them. He was an oak of a man: not over tall, but solid as a crag, and barreled with flesh, bone, and muscle.

His face was round and polished; blue eyes crinkled to the humor of his mouth. A tweed jacket strained across his back, and his legs, curved like the timbers of an old house, were clad in breeches, which tucked into thick woolen stockings just above the swelling calves. A felt hat, old and formless, was on his head, and hobnailed boots struck sparks from the platform as he walked.

"Hello! I'm thinking you mun be Colin and Susan." His voice was gusty and high-pitched, yet mellow, like an autumn gale.

"That's right," said Colin. "And are you Mr. Mossock?"

"I am—but we'll have none of your 'Mr. Mossock,' if you please. Gowther's my name. Now come on, let's be having you. Bess is getting us some supper, and we're not home yet."

He picked up their cases, and they made their way down the steps to the station yard, where there stood a green farm cart with high red wheels, and between the shafts was a white horse, with shaggy mane and fetlock.

"Eh up, Scamp!" said Gowther as he heaved the cases into the back of the cart. A brindled mongrel, which had been asleep on a rug, stood and eyed the children warily while they climbed to the seat. Gowther took his place between them, and away they drove under the station bridge on the last stage of their travels.

They soon left the village behind and were riding down a tree-bordered lane between fields. They talked of this and that, and the children were gradually accepted by Scamp, who came and thrust his head onto the seat between Susan and Gowther. Then, "What on earth's *that*?" said Colin.

They had just rounded a corner: before them, rising abruptly out of the fields a mile away, was a long-backed hill. It was high, and somber, and black. On the extreme right-hand flank, outlined against the sky, were the towers and spires of big houses showing above the trees, which covered much of the hill like a blanket.

"Yon's th'Edge," said Gowther. "Six hundred feet high and three mile long. You'll have some grand times theer, I con tell you. Folks think as how Cheshire's flat as a poncake, and so it is for the most part, but not wheer we live!"

Nearer they came to the Edge, until it towered above them, then they turned to the right along a road which kept to the foot of the hill. On one side lay the fields, and on the other the steep slopes. The trees came right down to the road, tall beeches which seemed to be whispering to each other in the breeze.

"It's a bit creepy, isn't it?" said Susan.

"Aye, theer's some as reckons it is, but you munner always listen to what folks say.

"We're getting close to Alderley village now, sithee: we've not come the shortest way, but I dunner care much for the main road, with its clatter and smoke, nor does Prince here. We shanner be going reet into the village; you'll see more of yon when we do our shopping of a Friday. Now here's wheer we come to a bit of steep."

They were at a crossroad. Gowther swung the cart

9

around to the left, and they began to climb. On either side were the walled gardens of the houses that covered the western slope of the Edge. It was very steep, but the horse plodded along until, quite suddenly, the road leveled out, and Prince snorted and quickened his pace.

"He knows his supper's waiting on him, dunner thee, lad?"

They were on top of the Edge now, and through gaps in the trees they caught occasional glimpses of lights twinkling on the plain far below. Then they turned down a narrow lane which ran over hills and hollows and brought them, at the last light of day, to a small farmhouse lodged in a fold of the Edge. It was built around a framework of black oak, with white plaster showing between the gnarled beams: there were diamond-patterned, lamp-yellow windows and a stone-flagged roof: the whole building seemed to be a natural part of the hillside, as if it had grown there. This was the end of the children's journey; Highmost Redmanhey, where a Mossock had farmed for three centuries and more.

"Hurry on in," said Gowther. "Bess'll be waiting supper for us. I'm just going to give Prince his oats."

Bess Mossock, before her marriage, had been nurse to the children's mother; and although it was all of twelve years since their last meeting they still wrote to each other from time to time and sent gifts at Christmas. So it was to Bess that their mother had turned when she had been called to join her husband abroad for six months, and Bess, ever the

10

nurse, had been happy to offer what help she could. "And it'll do this owd farmhouse a world of good to have a couple of childer brighten it up for a few months."

She greeted the children warmly, and after asking how their parents were, she took them upstairs and showed them their rooms.

When Gowther came in they all sat around the table in the broad, low-ceilinged kitchen where Bess served up a monstrous Cheshire pie. The heavy meal, on top of the strain of traveling, could have only one effect, and before long Colin and Susan were falling asleep on their chairs. So they said good night and went upstairs to bed, each carrying a candle, for there was no electricity at Highmost Redmanhey.

"Gosh, I'm tired!"

"Oh, me too!"

"This looks all right, doesn't it?"

"Mm."

"Glad we came now, aren't you?"

"Ye-es. . . ."

2

THE EDGE

"IF YOU LIKE," said Gowther at breakfast, "we've time for a stroll round before Sam comes, then we'll have to get in that last load of hay while the weather holds, for we could have thunder today as easy as not."

Sam Harlbutt, a lean young man of twenty-four, was Gowther's laborer, and a craftsman with a pitchfork. That morning he lifted three times as much as Colin and Susan combined, and with a quarter of the effort. By eleven o'clock the stack was complete, and they lay in its shade and drank rough cider out of an earthenware jar.

Later, at the end of the midday meal, Gowther asked the children if they had any plans for the afternoon.

"Well," said Colin, "if it's all right with you, we thought we'd like to go in the woods and see what there is there."

"Good idea! Sam and I are going to mend the pig-cote wall, and it inner a big job. You go and enjoy yourselves. But when you're up th'Edge see as you dunner venture down ony caves you might find, and keep an eye open for holes in the ground. Yon place is riddled with tunnels and

12

shafts from the owd copper mines. If you went down theer and got lost that'd be the end of you, for even if you missed falling down a hole you'd wander about in the dark until you upped and died."

"Thanks for telling us," said Colin. "We'll be careful."

"Tea's at five o'clock," said Bess.

"And think on you keep away from them mineholes!" Gowther called after them as they went out of the gate.

It was strange to find an inn there on that road. Its white walls and stone roof had nestled into the woods for centuries, isolated, with no other house in sight: a village inn, without a village. Colin and Susan came to it after a mile and a half of dust and wet tar in the heat of the day. It was named The Wizard, and above the door was fixed a painted sign which held the children's attention. The painting showed a man, dressed like a monk, with long white hair and beard: behind him a figure in old-fashioned peasant garb struggled with the reins of a white horse which was rearing on its hind legs. In the background were trees.

"I wonder what all that means," said Susan. "Remember to ask Gowther—he's bound to know."

They left the shimmering road for the green wood, and The Wizard was soon lost behind them as they walked among fir and pine, oak, ash, and silver birch, along tracks through bracken, and across sleek hummocks of grass. There was no end to the peace and beauty. And then, abruptly, they came upon a stretch of rock and sand from which the heat vibrated as if from an oven. To the north, the Cheshire plain spread before them like a green and yellow patchwork quilt dotted with toy farms and houses. Here the Edge dropped steeply for several hundred feet, while away to their right the country rose in folds and wrinkles until it joined the bulk of the Pennines, which loomed eight miles away through the haze.

The children stood for some minutes, held by the splendor of the view. Then Susan, noticing something closer to hand, said, "Look here! This must be one of the mines."

Almost at their feet a narrow trench sloped into the rock.

"Come on," said Colin, "there's no harm in going down a little way—just as far as the daylight reaches."

Gingerly they walked down the trench, and were rather disappointed to find that it ended in a small cave, shaped roughly like a discus, and full of cold, damp air. There were no tunnels or shafts: the only thing of note was a round hole in the roof, about a yard across, which was blocked by an oblong stone.

"Huh!" said Colin. "There's nothing dangerous about *this*, anyway."

All through the afternoon Colin and Susan roamed up and down the wooded hillside and along the valleys of the Edge, sometimes going where only the tall beech stood, and in such places all was still. On the ground lay dead leaves, nothing more: no grass or bracken grew; winter seemed to linger there among the gray, green beeches. When the children came out of such a wood it was like coming into a garden from a musty cellar.

In their wanderings they saw many caves and openings in the hill, but they never explored further than the limits of daylight.

Just as they were about to turn for home after a climb from the foot of the Edge, the children came upon a stone trough into which water was dripping from an overhanging cliff, and high in the rock was carved the face of a bearded man, and underneath was engraved:

DRINK OF THIS
AND TAKE THY FILL
FOR THE WATER FALLS
BY THE WIZHARDS WILL

"The wizard again!" said Susan. "We really must find out from Gowther what all this is about. Let's go straight home now and ask him. It's probably nearly teatime, anyway."

They were within a hundred yards of the farm when a car overtook them and pulled up sharply. The driver, a woman, got out and stood waiting for the children. She looked about forty-five years old, was powerfully built ("fat" was the word Susan used to describe her), and her head rested firmly on her shoulders without appearing to have much of a neck at all. Two lines ran from either side

15

of her nose to the corners of her wide, thin-lipped mouth, and her eyes were rather too small for her broad head. Strangely enough, her legs were thin and spindly, so that in outline she resembled a well-fed sparrow, but again that was Susan's description.

All this Colin and Susan took in as they approached the car, while the driver eyed them up and down more obviously.

"Is this the road to Macclesfield?" she said when the children came up to her.

"I'm afraid I don't know," said Colin. "We've only just come to stay here."

"Oh? Then you'll want a lift. Jump in!"

"Thanks," said Colin, "but we're living at this next farm."

"Get into the back."

"No, really. It's only a few yards."

"Get in!"

"But we . . ."

The woman's eyes glinted and the color rose in her cheeks.

"You—will—get—into—the back!"

"Honestly, it's not worth the bother! We'd only hold you up."

The woman drew breath through her teeth. Her eyes rolled upwards and the lids came down until only an unpleasant white line showed; and then she began to whisper to herself.

Colin felt most uncomfortable. They could not just walk

16

off and leave this peculiar woman in the middle of the road, yet her manner was so embarrassing that he wanted to hurry away, to disassociate himself from her strangeness.

"*Omptator,*" said the woman.

"I . . . beg your pardon."

"*Lapidator.*"

"I'm sorry . . ."

"*Somniator.*"

"Are you . . . ?"

"*Qui libertar opera facitis . . .*"

"I'm not much good at Latin. . . ."

Colin wanted to run now. She must be mad. He could not cope. His brow was damp with sweat, and pins and needles were taking all awareness out of his body.

Then, close at hand, a dog barked loudly. The woman gave a suppressed cry of rage and spun around. The tension broke; and Colin saw that his fingers were around the handle of the car door, and the door was half-open.

"Howd thy noise, Scamp," said Gowther sharply.

He was crossing the road opposite the farm gate, and Scamp stood a little way up the hill, nearer the car, snarling nastily.

"Come on! Heel!"

Scamp slunk unwillingly back toward Gowther, who waved to the children and pointed to the house to show that tea was ready.

"Th—that's Mr. Mossock," said Colin. "He'll be able to tell you the way to Macclesfield."

"No doubt!" snapped the woman. And, without another word, she threw herself into the car, and drove away.

"Well!" said Colin. "What was all that about? She must be off her head! I thought she was having a fit! What do you think was up with her?"

Susan made no comment. She gave a wan smile and shrugged her shoulders, but it was not until Colin and she were at the farm gate that she spoke.

"I don't know," she said. "It may be the heat, or because we've walked so far, but all the time you were talking to her I thought I was going to faint. But what's so strange is that my Tear has gone all misty."

Susan was fond of her Tear. It was a small piece of crystal, shaped like a raindrop, and had been given to her by her mother, who had had it mounted in a socket fastened to a silver chain bracelet which Susan always wore. It was a flawless stone, but, when she was very young, Susan had discovered that if she held it in a certain way, so that it caught the light just . . . so, she could see, deep in the heart of the crystal, miles away, or so it seemed, a twisting column of blue fire, always moving, never ending, alive, and very beautiful.

Bess Mossock clapped her hands in delight when she saw the Tear on Susan's wrist. "Oh, if it inner the Bridestone! And after all these years!"

Susan was mystified, but Bess went on to explain that "yon pretty dewdrop" had been given to her by her mother, who had had it from *her* mother, and so on, till its origin and the meaning of the name had become lost among the distant generations. She had given it to the children's mother because "it always used to catch the childer's eyes, and thy mother were no exception!"

At this, Susan's face fell. "Well then," she said, "it must go back to you now, because it's obviously a family heirloom and . . ."

"Nay, nay, lass! Thee keep it. I've no childer of my own, and thy mother was the same as a daughter to me. I con see as how it's in good hands."

So Susan's Tear had continued to sparkle at her wrist until that moment at the car, when it had suddenly clouded over, the color of whey.

"Oh, hurry up, Sue!" said Colin over his shoulder. "You'll feel better after a meal. Let's go and find Gowther."

"But, Colin!" cried Susan, holding up her wrist. She was about to say, "Do look!" but the words died in her throat, for the crystal now winked at her as pure as it had ever been.

3

MAGGOT-BREED OF YMIR

"AND WHAT DID owd Selina Place want with you?" said Gowther at tea.

"Selina Place?" said Colin. "Who's she?"

"You were talking to her just before you came in, and it's not often you see her bothering with folks."

"But how do you know her? She seemed to be a stranger round here, because she stopped to ask the way to Macclesfield."

"She did *what?*. But that's daft! Selina Place has lived in Alderley for as long as I con remember."

"She *has?*"

"Aye, hers is one of the big houses on the back hill—a rambling barn of a place it is, stuck on the edge of a cliff. She lives alone theer with what are supposed to be three dogs, but they're more like wolves, to my way of thinking, though I conner rightly say as I've ever seen them. She never takes them out with her. But I've heard them howling of a winter's night, and it's a noise I shanner forget in a hurry!

20

"And was that all she wanted? Just to know how to get to Macclesfield?"

"Yes. Oh, and she seemed to think that because we'd only recently come to live here we'd want a lift. But as soon as she saw you she jumped into the car and drove away. I think she's not quite all there."

"Happen you'd best have a word with yon," said Bess. "It all sounds a bit rum to me. I think she's up to summat."

"Get away with your bother! Dick Thornicroft's always said as she's a bit cracked, and it looks as though he's reet. Still, it's as well to keep clear of the likes of her, and I shouldner accept ony lifts, if I were you.

"Now then, from what you tell me, I con see as how you've been a tidy step this afternoon, so let's start near the beginning and then we shanner get ourselves lost. Well, yon place wheer you say theer was such a grand view is Stormy Point, and the cave with the hole in the roof is the Devil's Grave. If you run round theer three times widdershins Owd Nick's supposed to come up and fetch you."

And so all through their meal, Gowther entertained Colin and Susan with stories and explanations of the things they had seen in their wanderings, and at last, after frequent badgering, he turned to the subject of the wizard.

"I've been saving the wizard till the end. Yon's quite a long story, and now tea's finished I con talk and you con listen and we needner bother about owt else."

And Gowther told Colin and Susan the legend of Alderley.

21

"Well, it seems as how theer was once a farmer from Mobberley as had a milk-white mare. . . .

". . . and from that day to this no one has ever seen the gates or the wizard again."

"Is that a *true* story?" said Colin.

"Theer's some as reckons it is. But if it did happen it was so long ago that even the place wheer the iron gates are supposed to be has been forgotten. I say yon's nobbut a legend: but it makes fair telling after a good meal."

"Yes," said Susan, "but you know, our father has always said that there's no smoke without a fire."

"Aye, happen he's getten summat theer!" laughed Gowther.

The meal over, Colin and Susan went with Gowther to take some eggs to an old widow who lived in a tiny cottage a little beyond the farm boundary. And when they were returning across the Riddings, which was the name of the steep hill-field above Highmost Redmanhey, Gowther pointed to a large black bird that was circling above the farmyard.

"Hey! Sithee yon carrion crow! I wonder what he's after. If he dunner shift himself soon I'll take my shotgun to him. We dunner want ony of his sort round here, for they're a reet menace in the lambing season."

Early in the evening Colin, who had been very taken with the legend of the wizard, suggested another walk on the Edge, this time to find the iron gates.

22

"Aye, well I wish you luck! You're not the first to try, and I dunner suppose you'll be the last."

"Take your coats with you," said Bess. "It gets chilly on the top at this time o' day."

Colin and Susan roamed all over Stormy Point, and beyond, but there were so many rocks and boulders, any of which could have hidden the gates, that they soon tired of shouting "Abracadabra!" and "Open, Sesame!" and instead lay down to rest upon a grassy bank just beneath the crest of a spur of the Edge, and watched the sun drop toward the rim of the plain.

"I think it's time we were going, Colin," said Susan when the sun had almost disappeared. "If we don't reach the road before dark we could easily lose our way."

"All right: but let's go back to Stormy Point along the other side of this ridge, just for a change. We've not been over there yet."

He turned, and Susan followed him over the crest of the hill into the trees.

Once over the ridge, they found themselves in a dell, bracken and boulder filled, and edged with rocks, in which were cracks, and fissures, and small caves; and before them a high-vaulted beech wood marched steeply down into the dusk. The air was still and heavy, as though waiting for thunder; the only sound the concentrated whine of mosquitoes; and the thick, sweet smell of bracken and flies was everywhere.

23

"I . . . I don't like this place, Colin," said Susan: "I feel that we're being watched."

Colin did not laugh at her as he might normally have done. He, too, had that feeling between the shoulder blades; and he could easily have imagined that something was moving among the shadows of the rocks; something that managed to keep out of sight. So he gladly turned to climb back to the path.

They had moved barely a yard up the dell when Colin stopped and laughed.

"Look! Somebody *is* watching us!"

Perched on a rock in front of them was a bird. Its head was thrust forward, and it stared unwinkingly at the two children.

"It's the carrion crow that was round the farm after tea!" cried Susan.

"Talk sense! How can you tell it's the same one? There are probably dozens of them about here."

All the same, Colin did not like the way the bird sat hunched there so tensely, almost eagerly: and they had to pass it if they wanted to regain the path. He took a step forward, waved his arms in the air, and cried "Shoo!" in a voice that sounded woefully thin and unfrightening.

The crow did not move.

Colin and Susan moved forward, longing to run, but held by the crow's eye. And as they reached the center of the dell the bird gave a loud, sharp croak. Immediately a cry answered from among the rocks, and out of the

24

shadows on either side of the children rose a score of out-landish figures.

They stood about three feet high and were man-shaped, with thin, wiry bodies and limbs, and broad, flat feet and hands. Their heads were large, having pointed ears, round saucer eyes, and gaping mouths which showed teeth. Some had pug-noses, others thin snouts reaching to their chins. Their hides were generally of a fish-white color, though some were black, and all were practically hairless. Some held coils of black rope, while out of one of the caves advanced a group carrying a net woven in the shape of a spider's web.

For a second the children were rooted: but only for a second. Instinct took control of their wits. They raced back along the dell and flung themselves through the gap into the beech wood. Fingers clawed, and ropes hissed like snakes, but they were through and plunging down the slope in a flurry of dead leaves.

"Stop, Sue!" yelled Colin.

He realized that their only hope of escape lay in reaching open ground and the path that led from Stormy Point to the road, where their longer legs might outdistance their pursuers', and even that seemed a slim chance.

"Stop, Sue! We must . . . not go . . . down . . . any farther! Find . . . Stormy Point . . . somehow!"

All the while he was looking for a recognizable land-mark, since in the fear and dusk he had lost his bearings, and all he knew was that their way lay uphill and not down.

25

Then, through the trees, he saw what he needed. About a hundred feet above them and to their right a tooth-shaped boulder stood against the sky: its distinctive shape had caught his eye when they had walked past it *along a track coming from Stormy Point!*

"That boulder! Make for that boulder!"

Susan looked where he was pointing, and nodded.

They began to flounder up the hill, groping for firm ground with hands and feet beneath the knee-high sea of dead leaves. Their plunge had taken them diagonally across the slope, and their upward path led away from the dell, otherwise they would not have survived.

The others had come skimming lightly down over the surface of the leaves, and had found it difficult to check their speed when they saw the quick change of direction. Now they scurried across to intercept the children, bending low over the ground as they ran.

Slowly Colin and Susan gained height until they were at the same level as the pursuit, then above it, and the danger of being cut off from the path was no longer with them. But their lead was a bare ten yards, and shortening rapidly, until Colin's fingers, scrabbling beneath the leaves, closed around something firm. It was a fallen branch, still bushy with twigs, and he tore it from the soil, and swung it straight into the leaders, who went clamoring, head over heels, into those behind in a tangle of ropes and nets.

This gained Colin and Susan precious yards and seconds, though their flight was still nightmare; for unseen twigs rolled beneath their feet, and leaves dragged leadenly about their knees. But at last they pulled themselves onto the path.

"Come on, Sue!" Colin gasped. "Run for it! They're . . . not far . . . behind . . . now!"

The children drew energy from their fear. Above their heads a bird cried harshly three times, and at once the air was filled with the beating of a gong. The sound seemed to come from a distance, yet it was all about them, in the air and under the ground.

Then they ran clear of the trees and onto Stormy Point. But their relief was short-lived; for whereas till that moment they had been fleeing from twenty or so, they were now confronted with several hundred of the creatures as they came out of the Devil's Grave like ants from a nest.

Colin and Susan halted: gone was their last hope of reaching the road: the way was blocked to the front and rear: on their left was the grim beech wood: to the right an almost sheer slope dropped between pines into a valley. But at least there was no known danger there, so the children turned their faces that way and fled, stumbling and slithering down a sandy path, till at last they landed at the bottom—only to splash knee-deep in the mud and leaf-mold of the swamp that sprawled unseen down the opposite wall of the valley and out across the floor.

They lurched forward a few paces, spurred on by the sound of what was following all too close behind, but then Susan staggered and collapsed against a fallen tree.

"I can't go on!" she sobbed. "My legs won't move."

"Oh yes you *can!* Only a few more yards!"

Colin had spotted a huge boulder sticking out of the swamp a little way up the hill from where they were, and, if only they could reach it, it would offer more protection than their present position, which could hardly be worse. He grabbed his sister's arm and dragged her through the mud to the base of the rock.

"Now climb!"

And, while Susan hauled herself up to the flat summit, Colin put his back to the rock, like a fox at bay turning to face the hunt.

The edge of the swamp was a mass of bodies. The rising moon shone on their leathery hides and was reflected in their eyes. Colin could see white shapes spreading out on either side to encircle the rock: they were in no hurry now, for they knew that escape was impossible.

Colin climbed after his sister. He ached in every muscle and was trembling with fatigue.

When the circle was complete the creatures began to advance across the swamp, moving easily over the mire on their splayed feet. Ever closer they came, till the rock was surrounded.

From all sides at once the ropes came snaking through the air, as soft as silk, as strong as iron, and clung to the children as though coated with glue; so that in no time at all Colin and Susan fell helpless beneath the sticky coils, and over them swarmed the mob, pinching and poking, and binding and trussing, until the children lay with only their heads exposed, like two cocoons upon the rock.

But as they were being hoisted onto bony shoulders it seemed as though a miracle happened. There was a flash, and the whole rock was lapped about by a lake of blue fire. The children could feel no heat, but their captors fell, hissing and spitting, into the swamp, and the ropes charred and crumbled into ash, while pandemonium broke loose through all the assembly.

Then, from the darkness above, a voice rang out.

"Since when have men-children grown so mighty that you must needs meet two with hundreds? Run, maggot-breed of Ymir, ere I lose my patience!"

The crowd had fallen silent at the first sound of that voice, and now it drew back slowly, snarling and blinking in the blue light, wavered, turned, and fled. The dazed children listened to the rushing feet as though in a dream: soon there was only the rattle of stones on the opposite slope; then nothing. The cold flames about the rock flickered and died. The moon shone peacefully upon the quiet valley.

And as their eyes grew accustomed to this paler light the children saw standing on a path beneath a cliff some way above them an old man, taller than any they had ever known, and thin. He was clad in a white robe, his hair and beard were white, and in his hand was a white staff. He was looking at Colin and Susan, and, as they sat upright, he spoke again, but this time there was no anger in his voice.

29

"Come quickly, children, lest there be worse than svarts abroad; for indeed I smell much evil in the night. Come, you need not fear me."

He smiled and stretched out his hand. Colin and Susan climbed down from the rock and squelched their way up to join him. They were shivering in spite of their coats and recent exertions.

"Stay close to me. Your troubles are over, though I fear it may be only for this night, but we must take no risks."

And he touched the cliff with his staff. There was a hollow rumble, and a crack appeared in the rock, through which a slender ray of light shone. The crack widened to reveal a tunnel leading down into the earth: it was lit by a soft light, much the same as that which had scattered the mob in the swamp.

The old man herded Colin and Susan into the tunnel, and, as soon as they were past the threshold, the opening closed behind them, shutting out the night and its fears.

The tunnel was quite short, and soon they came to a door. The children stood aside while the old man fumbled with the lock.

"Where High Magic fails, oak and iron may yet prevail," he said. "Ah! That has it! Now enter, and be refreshed."

4

THE FUNDINDELVE

THEY WERE in a cave, sparsely but comfortably furnished. There was a long wooden table in the center, and a few carved chairs, and in one corner lay a pile of animal skins. Through the middle of the cave a stream of water babbled in the channel it had cut in the sandstone floor, and as it disappeared under the cave wall it formed a pool, into which the old man dipped two bronze cups, and offered them to Colin and Susan.

"Rest," he said, pointing to the heap of skins, "and drink of this."

The children sank down upon the bed and sipped the ice-cold water. And at the first draught their tiredness vanished, and a warmth spread through their limbs: their befuddled shock-numbed brains cleared, their spirits soared.

"Oh," cried Susan, as she gazed at their surroundings as though seeing them for the first time, "this can't be real! We *must* be dreaming. Colin, how do we wake up?"

But Colin was staring at the old man, and seemed not to have heard. He saw an old man, true, but one whose body was as firm and upright as a youth's; whose keen, gray eyes were full of the sadness of the wise; whose mouth, though stern, was kind, and capable of laughter.

"Then the legend *is* true," said Colin.

"It is," said the wizard. "And I would it were not; for that was a luckless day for me.

"But enough of my troubles. We must discover now what is in you to draw the attentions of the svart-alfar, since it is indeed strange that men-children should cause them such concern."

"Oh please," interrupted Susan, "this is so bewildering! Can't you tell us first what's been happening and what those things were in the marsh? We don't even know who you are, though I suppose you must be the wizard."

The old man smiled. "Forgive me. In my disquiet I had forgotten that you have seen much that has been unknown to you.

"Who am I?" I have had many names among many peoples through the long ages of the earth, and of those names some may not now be spoken, or would be foreign to your tongue; but you shall call me Cadellin, after the fashion of the men of Elthan, in the days to come, for I believe our paths will run together for a while.

"The creatures you encountered are of the goblin race— the svart-alfar, in their own tongue. They are a cowardly people, night-loving, and sun-loathing, much given to throttlings in dark places, and seldom venturing above

32

ground unless they have good cause. They have no magic, and so, alone, are no danger to me; but it would have fared ill with you had I not known their alarm echoing through the hollow hill.

"And now you must tell me who *you* are, and what it is that has brought you into such danger this night."

Colin and Susan gave an account of the events leading to their arrival in Alderley, and of their movements since.

"And this afternoon," said Colin finally, "we explored the Edge, and spent the rest of the day on the farm until we came here again about half past seven, so I don't see that we can have done anything to attract *any*body's attention."

"Hm," said Cadellin thoughtfully. "Now tell me what happened this evening, for at present I can find no reason in this."

The children told the story of their flight and capture, and when they had finished the wizard was silent for some time.

"This is indeed puzzling," he said at last. "The crow was sent to arrange your taking, and I do not have to guess by whom it was sent. But *why* the morthbrood should be concerned with you defeats me utterly: yet I must discover this reason, both for your safety and my own, for my destruction is their aim, and somehow I fear you could advance them in their work. Still, perhaps the next move will tell us more, for they will soon hear of what took place this night, and will be much alarmed. But I shall give you what

33

protection I can, and you will find friends as well as enemies in these woods."

"But why are *you* in danger?" said Susan. "And who are the—what was it?—morthbrood?"

"Ah, that is a long story for this hour, and one of which I am ashamed. But it is also, I suppose, one that you must hear. So, if you are rested, let us go together, and I shall show you part of the answer to your question."

Cadellin led the children out of the cave and down a long winding tunnel into the very heart of the hill. And as they went the air grew colder and the strange light fiercer, turning from blue to white, until at last they came into a long, low cavern. An echoing sigh, like waves slowly rippling on a summer shore, rose and fell upon the air: and before the children's eyes were the sleeping knights in their silver armor, each beside his milk-white mare, just as Gowther had described them in the legend, their gentle breathing filling the cave with its sweet sound. And all around and over the motionless figures the cold, white flames played silently.

In the middle of the cave the floor rose in the shape of a natural, tomb-like couch of stone; and here lay a knight comelier than all his fellows. His head rested upon a helmet enriched with jewels and circlets of gold, and its crest was a dragon. By his side was placed a naked sword, and on the blade was the image of two serpents in gold, and so brightly did the blade gleam that it was as if two flames of fire started from the serpents' heads.

34

"Long years ago," said Cadellin, "beyond the memory or books of men, Nastrond, the Great Spirit of Darkness, rode forth in war upon the plain. But there came against him a mighty king and Nastrond fell. He cast off his earth-shape and fled into the Abyss of Ragnarok, and all men rejoiced, thinking that evil had vanished from the world forever: yet the king knew in his heart that this could never be.

"So he called together a great assembly of wizards and wise men and asked what should be done to guard against the enemy's return. And it was prophesied that, when the day should come, Nastrond must be victorious, for there would be none pure enough to withstand him since, by that time, he would have put a little of himself into the hearts of all men. Even now, it was said, he was pouring black thoughts from his lair in Ragnarok, and these would flow unceasingly about mankind until the strongest were tainted and he had a foothold in every mind.

"Yet there was hope. For the world might still be saved if a band of warriors, pure in heart, and brave, could defy him in his hour and compel him to sink once more into the Abyss. Their strength would not be in numbers, but in purity and valor. And so was devised the following plan.

"The king chose the worthiest of his knights, and went with them to Fundindelve, the ancient dwarf-halls, where they were put into enchanted sleep. This done, the most powerful magicians of the age began to weave a spell. Day and night they worked together, pausing for neither food

35

nor sleep, and, at the end, Fundindelve was guarded by the strongest magic the world has known, magic that would stay the sleeping warriors from growing old or weak, and that no evil could ever break.

"The heart of the magic was sealed with Firefrost, the weirdstone of Brisingamen, and it and the warriors became my charge. Here I must stay, forever keeping watch, until the time shall come for me to rouse the Sleepers and send them forth against the malice of Nastrond."

"But, Cadellin," asked Susan, "in these days how can you hope to win a fight with only a hundred and forty men on horseback?"

"Ah," said the wizard, "you must remember that the hour of Nastrond is not yet at hand. It was prophesied that these few could prove his desolation, and I have faith: the wheel may turn full circle ere that day will come."

This cryptic reply was hardly satisfying, but by the time Susan had tried to make sense of it and found that she could not, the wizard had resumed his tale.

"Now it happened that, at the Sealing of Fundindelve, there were not more than one hundred and thirty-nine pure white mares in the prime of life, to be found anywhere. Therefore I was forced to wait for that one horse to complete my company, and when at last such a horse came my way, I little knew that it would be so dearly bought.

"But now I must leave this matter and speak of Nastrond. Word of what we had done at Fundindelve soon reached him, and he was both angry and afraid; yet his black art was of no avail against our stronghold. So he too devised a plan.

"In the next chamber to that of the Sleepers had been stored jewels and precious metals for the use of the king to help put right the ills of the world, if he should conquer Nastrond. This treasure, since it lay in Fundindelve, was safe as long as the spell remained unbroken; and although Nastrond had no thought for the treasure, he did desire most furiously to break the spell, for, if this were achieved, the Sleepers would wake and become normal men, who would grow old, and die, and pass away centuries before his return, since there would no longer be magic left upon the earth powerful to hold them once more ageless in Fundindelve.

"To this end he summoned the witches and warlocks of the morthbrood, and the lords of the svart-alfar, together with many of his own ministers, and put greed and a craving for riches in their hearts by telling them of the treasure that would be theirs if they could only reach it. And from that hour they have striven to find a way to break the spell. At first I had no need to fear, for the sorcery of the morthbrood, though powerful, and the hammers and shovels of svarts could have no effect where the art of Nastrond had failed. But then, on the day that I found the last white mare, disaster fell upon me.

"This light around us is the magic that guards all here, and its flames are torment to the followers of Nastrond: and the source of the magic, as I have said, rests in the stone Firefrost. While Firefrost remains, and there is light in Fundindelve, the Sleepers lie here in safety. Yet each day I dread that I shall see the flames tremble and give way to shadows, and hear the murmur of men roused from sleep, and the neigh of horses. For I have lost the weirdstone of Brisingamen!"

Cadellin's voice trembled with rage and shame as he spoke, and he crashed the butt of his staff against the rock floor.

"Lost it?" cried Susan. "You can't have done! I mean, if it's a special stone it should be easy to find if it's lying around somewhere in here . . . shouldn't it?"

The wizard smiled grimly. "But it is *not* here. Of that, at least, I am certain. Come, and I shall show you proof of what I say."

He beckoned the children toward an opening in the wall and into a short tunnel not more than thirty feet in length, and halfway down Cadellin stopped before a bowl-shaped recess about six inches high and a yard above the level of the floor.

"There is the throne of Firefrost," he said, "and you will see that it is now vacant."

They passed through into a cavern similar to the last, and Colin and Susan halted in awe.

Here lay the treasure, piled in banks of jewels, and gold, and silver, which stretched away into the distance like sand dunes in a desert.

"Oh," gasped Susan, "how beautiful! Look at those colors!"

"You would not think them so beautiful," said Cadellin, "if you had run through your fingers every diamond, pearl, sapphire, amethyst, opal, carbuncle, garnet, topaz, emerald, and ruby in the whole of this all too spacious cave, in search of a stone that is not there!

"I spent five years laboring in this cave, and as many weeks scouring every gallery and path in Fundindelve, but without success. I can only think that that knave of a farmer was a greedier and more cunning rogue than he appeared, and that, as he followed me from here, laden as he was with wealth, his eyes fell upon the stone, and he slyly took it without a word. Perhaps he thought it was merely a pretty bauble, or he may even have seen me replace it after I had tethered his horse with sleep while he crammed his pockets here.

"Seldom have I need to visit these quarters, and it was a hundred years before I next came this way and found that the stone had gone. First I searched here; then I went out into the world to seek the farmer or his family. But, of course, by this time he was dead, and I could not trace his descendants; and although my quest was discreet the morthbrood came to hear of it, and they were not long in guessing the truth. Throughout the region of the plain they coursed, and even to the bleak uplands of the east, toward Ragnarok, but neither they nor the ferreting svarts found what they sought. Nor, for that matter, did I.

"Should Firefrost come into Nastrond's hand my danger would be great indeed; for although he is powerless against

39

the magic it contains, if he could destroy the stone then the magic, too, would die away.

"Firefrost was an ancient spellstone of great strength before the present magic was sealed within, and it would not readily suffer destruction: so while the light shines here I know that somewhere the stone still lives, and there is hope.

"There you have the story of my troubles, and, I trust, the answer to your questions. Now you must return to your home, for the hour is late and your friends will be anxious—and they may have ample cause for worry if we cannot solve this evening's problems soon!"

They went back into the Cave of the Sleepers, and from there climbed upwards by vast caverns till the way was blocked by a pair of iron gates, behind which the tunnel ended in a sheer rock wall. The wizard touched the gates with his staff, and slowly they swung open.

"These were wrought by dwarfs to guard their treasures from the thievish burrowings of svarts, but without magic they would be of little use against what seeks to enter now."

So saying, Cadellin laid his hand upon the wall, and a dark gap appeared in the blue rock, through which the night air flowed, cold and dew-laden.

It looked very black outside, and the memory of their recent fear made Colin and Susan unwilling to leave the light and safety of Fundindelve; but, keeping close to the wizard, they stepped through the gap, and stood once more beneath the trees on the hillside.

The gates and the opening closed behind them with a

sound that made the earth shake, and as they grew used to the moonlight the children saw that they were standing before the tooth of rock that they had striven to reach as they floundered in the depths of the beech wood, with svart-claws grasping at their heels.

Away to the left they could make out the shape of the ridge above the dell.

"That's where the svarts attacked us," said Colin, pointing.

"You do not surprise me!" laughed the wizard. "Saddlebole was ever a svart-warren; a good place to watch the sun set, indeed!"

They walked up the path to Stormy Point. All was quiet: just the gray rocks, and the moonlight. When they passed the dark slit of the Devil's Grave Colin and Susan instinctively huddled closer to the wizard, but nothing stirred within the blackness of the cave.

"Do svarts live in all the mines?" asked Susan.

"They do. They have their own warrens, but when men dug here they followed, hoping that Fundindelve would be revealed; and when the men departed they swarmed freely. Therefore you must keep away from the mines now, at all cost."

Cadellin took the children from Stormy Point along a broad track that cut straight through the wood as far as the open fields, where it turned sharply to twist along the meadow border skirting the woodland. This, the wizard said, was once an elf-road, and some of the old magic still

41

lingered. Svarts would not set foot on it, and the morth-brood would do so only if hard pressed, and then they could not bear to walk there for long. He told the children to use this road if they had need to visit him, and not to stray from it: for parts of the wood were evil, and very dangerous. "But then," he said, "you have already found that to be true!" It would be wiser, he thought, to stay away from the wood altogether, and on no account must they go out of doors once the sun had set.

The track came to an end by the side of The Wizard Inn, and they had gone barely a hundred yards from there when they heard the sound of hoofs, and around the corner ahead of them came the shape of a horse and cart, oil lamps flickering on either side.

"It's Gowther!"

"Do not speak of me!" said Cadellin.

"Oh, but . . ." began Susan. "But . . ."

But they were alone.

"Wey back!" called Gowther to Prince. "Hallo theer! Dunner you think it's a bit late to be looking for wizards? It's gone eleven o'clock, tha knows."

"Oh, we're sorry, Gowther," said Colin. "We didn't mean to be late, but we were lost, and stuck in a bog, and it took us a long time to find the road again."

He thought that this half-lie would be more readily accepted than the truth, and Cadellin obviously wanted to keep his existence a secret.

"Eh well, we'll say no more about it then; but think on

you're more careful in future, for with all them mine holes lying around, Bess was for having police and fire brigade out to look for you.

"Now up you come: if you've been trapesing round in Holywell bog you'll be wanting a bath, I reckon."

On reaching the farm Colin and Susan wasted no time in dragging off their muddy clothes and climbing into a steaming bathtub. From there they went straight to bed, and Bess, who had been fussing and clucking around like a hen with chicks, brought them bowls of hot, salted bread and milk.

The children were too tired to think, let alone talk, much about their experience, and as they drowsily snuggled down between the sheets all seemed to grow confused and vague: it was impossible to keep awake. Colin slid into a muddled world of express trains, and black birds, and bracken, and tunnels, and dead leaves, and horses.

"Oh gosh," he yawned, "which is which? Are there wizards and goblins? Or are we still at home? Must ask Sue about . . . about . . . oh . . . knights . . . ask Mum . . . don't believe in farmers . . . farm—no . . . witches . . . and . . . things . . . oh . . ."

He began, very quietly, to snore.

On the crest of the Riddings, staring down upon the farmhouse as it lay bathed in gossamer moonlight, was a dark figure, tall and gaunt: and on its shoulder crouched an ugly bird.

5

MICHING MALLECHO

THE NEXT DAY was cool and showery. The children slept late, and it was nine o'clock when they came down for breakfast.

"I thought it best to let you have a lie in this morning," said Bess. "You looked dead beat last neet; aye, and you're a bit pale now. Happen you'd do better to take things easy today, and not go gallivanting over the Edge."

"Oh, I think we've seen enough of the Edge for a day or two," said Susan. "It *was* rather tiring."

Breakfast was hardly over when a truck arrived from Alderley station with the children's bicycles and trunks, and Colin and Susan immediately set about the task of unpacking their belongings.

"What do you make of last night?" asked Susan when they were alone. "It doesn't seem possible, does it?"

"That's what I was wondering in bed: but we can't both have imagined it. The wizard *is* in a mess, isn't he? I shouldn't like to live by myself all the time and be on guard against things like those svarts."

44

"He said things *worse* than svarts, remember! I shouldn't have thought anything could be worse than those clammy hands and bulging eyes, and their flat feet splashing in the mud. If it's so, then I'm glad I'm not a wizard!"

They did not discuss their pursuit and rescue. It was too recent for them to think about it without trembling and feeling sick. So they talked mainly about the wizard and his story, and it was late afternoon before they had finished unpacking and had found a place for everything.

Colin and Susan went down to tea. Gowther was already at the table, talking to Bess.

"And a couple of rum things happened after dinner, too. First, I go into the barn for some sacks, and, bless me, if the place inner full of owls! I counted nigh on two dozen snoozing among the rafters—big uns, too. They mun be thinking we're sneyed out with mice, or summat. *I've* never seen owt like it.

"And then again, about an hour later, a feller comes up to me in Front Baguley, and he asks if I've a job for him. I didner like his looks at all. He was a midget, with long black hair and a beard, and skin like owd leather. He didner talk as if he came from round here, either—he was more Romany than owt else, to my way of thinking; and his clothes looked as though they'd been borrowed and slept in.

"Well, when I tell him I dunner need a mon, he looks fair put out, and he starts to tell me his hard luck story, and asks me to give him a break, but I give him his marching orders instead. He dunner argue: he just turns on his heel and stalks off, saying as I might regret treating him like this before long. He seemed in a fair owd paddy! All the same, I think Scamp had best have the run of the hen pen for a neet or two, just in case."

The wizard had told Colin and Susan to keep their windows closed, no matter how hot and stuffy their bedrooms might become, so the colder weather was not unwelcome, and they slept soundly enough that night.

Not so Gowther. The furious barking of Scamp woke him at three o'clock. It was the tone used for strangers, high-pitched and continuous, not the gruff outbursts that answered other dogs, birds, or the wind. Gowther scrambled into his clothes, seized his shotgun and lantern, which he had put ready to hand, and made for the door.

"I knew it! I knew it! The little blighter's after my chickens. I'll give him chickens!"

"Watch thy step, lad," said Bess. "You're bigger than he is, and that's all the more of thee for him to hit."

"I'll be all reet; but he wunner," said Gowther, and he clumped down the stairs and out into the farmyard.

Thick clouds hid the moon, there was little wind. The only sounds were the frantic clamor of the dog and the bumping of frightened, sleep-ridden hens.

Gowther shone his light into the pen. The wire netting was undamaged, and the gate locked. In the center of the lamp's beam stood Scamp. His hackles were up, in fact every hair along his spine seemed to be on end; his ears lay flat against his skull, and his eyes blazed yellow in the light. He was barking and snarling, almost screaming at times, and tearing the earth with stiff jerky movements of his legs. Gowther unfastened the gate.

"Wheer is he, boy? Go fetch him!"

Scamp came haltingly out of the pen, his lips curled hideously. Gowther was puzzled: he had expected him to come out like a rocket.

"Come on, lad! He'll be gone else!"

The dog ran backwards and forwards nervously, still barking, then he set off toward the field gate in a snarling glide, keeping his belly close to the ground, and disappeared into the darkness. A second later the snarl rose to a yelp, and he shot back into the light to land at Gowther's feet in a further welter of noise. He was trembling all over. His fury had been obvious all along, but now Gowther realized that, more than anything else, the dog was terrified.

"What's up, lad? What's frit thee, eh?" said Gowther gently as he knelt to calm the shivering animal. Then he stood up and went over toward the gate, his gun cocked, and shone the light into the field.

There was nothing wrong as far as he could see, but Scamp, though calmer, still foamed at his heels. Nothing wrong, yet there was something . . . wait! . . . he sniffed . . . was there? . . . yes! ! ! A cold, clammy air drifted against Gowther's face, and with it a smell so strange, so unwholesome, and unexpected that a knot of instinctive fear tightened in his stomach. It was the smell of stagnant

47

water and damp decay. It filled his nostrils and choked his lungs, and, for a moment, Gowther imagined that he was being sucked down into the depths of a black swamp, old and wicked in time. He swung around, gasping, wide-eyed, the hairs of his neck prickling erect. But on the instant the stench passed and was gone: he breathed pure night air once more.

"By gow, lad, theer's summat rum afoot toneet! That was from nowt local, choose how the wind blows. Come on, let's be having a scrat round."

He went first to the stable, where he found Prince stamping nervously, and covered with sweat.

"Wey, lad," said Gowther softly, and he ran his hands over the horse's quivering flanks. "Theer's no need to fret. Hush while I give thee a rub."

Prince gradually quieted down as Gowther rubbed him with a piece of dry sacking, and Scamp, too, was in a happier frame of mind. He carried his head high, and his din was reduced to a growl, threatening rather than nervous —as though trying to prove that he had never felt anything but aggressive rage all night.

Aye, thought Gowther, and yon's a dog as fears neither mon nor beast most days: I dunner like it one bit!

In the sheds he found the cows restless, but not as excited as Prince had been, for all their rolling eyes and snuffing nostrils.

"Well, theer's nowt here, Scamp: let's take a look at the barn."

They went into the outbuildings, and nowhere was there any hint of disturbance, nor did anything appear to have been tampered with.

"Aye, well everywheer seems reet enough now, onyroad," said Gowther, "so we'll have a quick peek round the house and mash a pot of tea, and then it'll be time to start milking. Eh dear, theer's no rest for the wicked!"

The sky was showing the first pale light of day as he crossed the farmyard: soon another morning would be here to drive away the fears of the night. Already Gowther was feeling a little ashamed of his moment of fear, and he was thankful that there had been no one else there to witness it. "Eh, it's funny how your imagination plays . . ." He stopped dead in his tracks, while Scamp pressed, whining, close to his legs.

Out of the blackness, far above Gowther's head, had come a single shriek, too harsh for human voice, yet more than animal.

For the second time that night Gowther's blood froze. Then, taking a deep breath, he strode quickly and purposefully toward the house, looking neither to the right nor to the left, neither up nor down, with Scamp not an inch from his heels. In one movement he lifted the latch, stepped across the threshold, closed the door, and shot the bolt home. Slowly he turned and looked down at Scamp.

"I dunner know about thee, lad, but I'm going to have a strong cup of tea."

He lit the paraffin lamp and put the kettle on the stove,

and while he waited for the water to boil he went from room to room to see that nothing was amiss here at least. All was quiet; though when he looked into Susan's room a sleepy voice asked what the time was and why Scamp had been making such a noise. Gowther said that a fox had been after the hens, or so he thought, but Scamp had frightened him off. He told a similar story to Bess.

". . . and he started barking at his own shadder, he was that excited."

"Aye? Then what is it as has made *thee* sweat like a cheese?" said Bess suspiciously.

"Well," said Gowther, confused, "I reckon it's a bit early in the day to be running round, at my age. But I'm not past mashing a pot of tea—er—I'll bring you one: kettle's boiling!"

Gowther sought the kitchen. It was never easy to keep anything from Bess, she knew him too well. But what could he say? That he, a countryman, had been frightened by a smell and a night bird? He almost blushed to think of it.

By the time he had made the tea, washed, and finished dressing, it was light outside and near milking time. The sun was breaking through the cloud. Gowther felt much better now.

He was halfway across the yard when he noticed the long, black feathers that lay scattered upon the cobblestones.

6

A RING OF STONES

Thursday at Highmost Redmanhey was always busy, for on top of the normal round of work Gowther had to make ready for the following day, when he would drive down to Alderley village to do the weekly shopping, and also to call on certain old friends and acquaintances whom he supplied with vegetables and eggs. So much of Thursday was taken up with selecting and cleaning the produce for Friday's marketing.

When all was done, Colin and Susan rode with Gowther to the wheelwright in the nearby township of Mottram St. Andrew to have a new spoke fitted to the cart. This occupied them until teatime, and afterwards Gowther asked the children if they would like to go with him down to Nether Alderley to see whether they could find their next meal in Radnor mere.

They set off across the fields, and shortly came to a wood. Here the undergrowth was denser than on most of the Edge, and contained quite a lot of bramble. High rhododendron bushes grew wild everywhere. The wood seemed full of birds. They sang in the trees, rustled in the thicket, and swam in the many quiet pools.

"I've just realized something," said Colin: "I felt the Edge was unusual, and now I know why. It's the . . ."

"Birds," said Gowther. "Theer is none. Not worth speaking of, onyroad. Flies, yes; but birds, no. It's always been like that, to my knowledge, and I conner think why it should be. You'd think, with all them trees and suchlike, you'd have as mony as you find here, but, considering the size of the place, theer's hardly a throstle to be found from Squirrel's Jump to Daniel Hill. Time's been when I've wandered round theer half the day, and seen nobbut a pair of jays, and that was in Clockhouse wood. No, it's very strange, when you come to weigh it up."

Their way took them through a jungle of rhododendron. The ground was boggy and choked with dead wood, and they had to duck under low branches and climb over fallen trees: but, somehow, Gowther managed to carry his rod and line through it all without a snag, and he even seemed to know where he was going.

Susan thought how unpleasant it would be to have to move quickly through such country.

"Gowther," she said, "are there any mines near here?"

"No, none at all, we're almost on the plain now, and the mines are over the other side of the hill, behind us. Why do you ask?"

"Oh, I just wondered."

52

The rhododendrons came to an end at the border of a mere, about half a mile long and a quarter wide.

"This is it," said Gowther, sitting down on a fallen trunk which stretched out over the water. "It's a trifle marshy, but we're not easy to reach here, as theer's some as might term this poaching. Now if you'll open yon basket and pass the tin with the bait in it, we can settle down and make ourselves comfortable."

After going out as far as he could along the tree to cast his rod, Gowther sat with his back against the roots and lit his pipe. Colin and Susan lay full length on the wrinkled bark and gazed into the mere.

Within two hours they had three perch between them, so they gathered in their tackle and headed for home, arriving well before dusk.

The following morning in Alderley village Susan went with Bess to the shops while Colin stayed to help Gowther with the vegetables. They all met again for a meal at noon, and afterwards climbed into the cart and went with Gowther on his round.

It was a hot day, and by four o'clock Colin and Susan were very thirsty, so Bess said that they ought to drop off for an ice cream and a lemonade.

"We've to go down Moss Lane," she said, "and we shanner be above half an hour; you stay and cool down a bit."

The children were soon in the village café, with their drinks before them. Susan was toying with her bracelet, and idly trying to catch the light so that she could see the blue heart of her Tear.

"It's always difficult to find," she said. "I never know when it's going to come right . . . ah . . . wait a minute . . . yes . . . got it! You know, it reminds me of the light in Fundin. . . ."

She looked at Colin. He was staring at her, openmouthed. They both dropped their eyes to Susan's wrist where her Tear gleamed so innocently.

"But it *couldn't* be!" whispered Colin. "Could it?"

"I don't . . . know. But how?"

But how?

"No, of course not!" said Colin. "The wizard would have recognized it as soon as he saw it, wouldn't he?"

Susan flopped back in her chair, releasing her pent-up breath in a long sigh. But a second later she was bolt upright, inarticulate with excitement.

"He couldn't have seen it! I—I was wearing my raincoat! Oh, *Colin* . . . ! !"

Though just as shaken as his sister, Colin was not content to sit and gape. Obviously they had to find out, and quickly, whether Susan was wearing Firefrost, or just a piece of crystal. If it *should* be Firefrost, and had been recognized by the wrong people, their brush with the svarts would at last make sense. How the stone came to be on Susan's wrist was another matter.

"We must find Cadellin at once," he said. "Because if this *is* Firefrost, the sooner he has it the better it will be for us all."

At that moment the cart drew up outside, and Gowther called that it was time to be going home.

The children tried hard to conceal their agitation, yet the leisurely pace Prince seemed to adopt on the "front" hill, as it was called locally, had them almost bursting with impatience.

"Bess," said Susan, "are you sure you can't remember anything else about the Bridestone? I want to find out as much as I can about it."

"Nay, lass, I've told you all as I know. My mother had it from her mother, and she always said as it had been passed down like that for I dunner know how many years. And I believe theer was some story about how it should never be shown to onybody outside the family for fear of bringing seven years' bad luck, but my mother didner go in much for superstition and that sort of claptrap."

"Have you always lived in Alderley?"

"Bless you, yes! I was born and bred in th'Hough," (she pronounced it "thuff") "but my mother was a Goostrey woman, and I believe before that her family had connections Mobberley way."

"Oh?"

Colin and Susan could hardly contain themselves.

"Gowther," said Colin, "before we come home, Sue and I want to go to Stormy Point; which is the nearest way?"

55

"What! Before you've had your teas?" exclaimed Bess.

"Yes, I'm afraid so. You see, it's something very important and secret, and we *must* go."

"You're not up to owt daft down the mines, are you?" said Gowther.

"Oh no," said Colin; "but, please, we must go. We'll be back early, and it doesn't matter about tea."

"Eh well, it'll be your stomachs as'll be empty! But think on, we dunner want to come looking for you at midneet.

"Your best way'll be to get off at the gamekeeper's lodge, and follow the main path till it forks by the owd quarry: then take the left hond path, and it'll bring you straight to Stormy Point."

They reached the top of the Edge, and after about quarter of a mile Gowther halted Prince before a cottage built of red sandstone and tucked in the fringe of the wood. Along the side of the cottage, at right angles to the road, a track disappeared among the trees in what Gowther said was the direction of Stormy Point.

The children jumped from the cart, and ran off along the track, while Gowther and Bess continued on their way, dwelling sentimentally on what it was to be young.

"Don't you think we'd better go by the path Cadellin told us to use? He said it was the only safe one, remember."

"We haven't time to go all that way round," said Colin; "we must show him your Tear as soon as we can. And anyway, Gowther says this is the path to Stormy Point, and it's broad daylight, so I don't see that we can come to any harm."

"Well, how are we going to find Cadellin when we're there?"

"We'll go straight to the iron gates and call him: being a wizard he's bound to hear . . . I hope. Still, we must try!"

They pressed deeper and deeper into the wood, and came to a level stretch of ground where the bracken thinned and gave place to rich turf, dappled with sunlight. And here, in the midst of so much beauty, they learned too late that wizards' words are seldom idle, and traps well sprung hold hard their prey.

Out of the ground on all sides swirled tongues of thick white mist, which merged into a rolling fog about the children's knees; it paused, gathered itself, and leaped upwards, blotting out the sun and the world of life and light.

It was too much for Susan. Her nerve failed her. All that mattered was to escape from this chill cloud and what it must contain. She ran blindly, stumbled a score of paces, then tripped, and fell full length upon the grass.

She was not hurt, but the jolt brought her to her senses: the jolt—and something else.

In falling, she had thrown her arms out to protect herself, and as her head cleared she realized that there was no earth beneath her fingers, only emptiness. She lay there, not daring to move.

"Sue, where are you?" It was Colin's voice, calling softly. "Are you all right?"

"I'm here. Be careful. I think I'm on the edge of a cliff, but I can't see."

"Keep still, then: I'll feel my way to you."

He crawled in the direction of Susan's voice, but even in that short distance he partly lost his bearing, and it was several minutes before he found his sister, and having done so, he wriggled cautiously alongside her.

The turf ended under his nose, and all beyond was a sea of gray. Colin felt around for a pebble, and dropped it over the edge. Three seconds passed before he heard it land.

"Good job you tripped, Sue! It's a long way down. This must be the old quarry. Now keep quiet a minute, and listen."

They strained their ears to catch the slightest sound, but there was nothing to be heard. They might have been the only living creatures on earth.

"We must go back to the path, Sue. And we've got to make as little noise as possible, because whatever it is that made this fog will be listening for us. If we don't find the path we may easily walk round in circles until nightfall, even supposing we're left alone as long as that.

"Let's get away from this quarry, for a start: there's no point in asking for trouble."

They stood up, and holding each other's hand, walked slowly back toward the path.

As the minutes went by, Susan grew more and more uneasy.

"Colin," she said at last, "I hadn't run more than a dozen steps, I'm sure, when I tripped, and we've been walking for a good five minutes. Do you think we're going the right way?"

"No, I don't. And I don't know which *is* the right way, so we'll have to hope for the best. We'll try to walk in a straight line, and perhaps we'll leave this fog behind."

But they did not. Either the mist had spread out over a wide area, or, as the children began to suspect, it was moving with them. They made very slow progress; every few paces they would stop and listen, but there was only the silence of the mist, and that was as unnerving as the sound of something moving would have been. Also, it was impossible to see for more than a couple of yards in any direction, and they were frightened of falling into a hidden shaft, or even the quarry, for they had lost all sense of direction by now.

The path seemed to have vanished; but, in fact, they had crossed it some minutes earlier without knowing. As they approached, the mist had gathered thickly about their feet, hiding the ground until the path was behind them.

After a quarter of an hour Colin and Susan were shivering uncontrollably as the dampness ate into their bones. Every so often the trunk of a pine tree would loom out of the mist, so that it seemed as though they were walking

59

through a pillared hall that had no beginning, and no end.

"We must be moving in circles, Colin. Let's change direction instead of trying to keep in a straight line."

"We couldn't be more lost than we are at present, so we may as well try it."

They could not believe their luck. Within half a minute they came upon an oak, and beyond that another. The fog was as dense as ever, but they knew that they were breaking fresh ground, and that was encouraging.

"Oh, I wish Cadellin would come," said Susan.

"That's an idea! Let's shout for help: he may hear us."

"But we'll give our position away."

"I don't think that matters anymore. Let's try, anyway."

"All right."

"One, two, three. Ca-dell-in! Help! Ca-dell-in! !"

It was like shouting in a padded cell. Their voices, flat and dead, soaked into the gray blanket.

"That can't have carried far," said Colin disgustedly. "Try again. One, two, three. Help! Ca-dell-in! Help! ! !"

"It's no use," said Susan; "he'll never hear us. We'll have to find our own way out."

"And we'll do that if we keep going at our own pace," said Colin. "If whatever caused this had intended to attack us it would have done so by now, wouldn't it? No, it wants to frighten us into rushing over a precipice or something like that. As long as we carry on slowly we'll be safe enough."

He was wrong, but they had no other plan.

For the next few minutes the children made their way in silence, Susan concentrating on the ground immediately in front, Colin alert for any sight or sound of danger.

All at once Susan halted.

"Hello, what's this?"

At their feet lay two rough-hewn boulders, and beyond them, on either side, could be seen the faint outline of others of a like size.

"What can they be? They look as though they've been put there deliberately, don't they?"

"Never mind," said Colin; "we mustn't waste time in standing around."

And they passed between the stones, only to stop short a couple of paces later, with despair in their hearts, cold as the east wind.

Susan's question was answered. They were in the middle of a ring of stones, and the surrounding low, dim shapes rose on the limit of vision as though marking the boundary of the world.

Facing the children were two stones, far bigger than the rest, and on one of the stones sat a figure, and the sight of it would have daunted a brave man.

For three fatal seconds the children stared, unable to think or move. And as they faltered, the jaws of the trap closed about them; for, like a myriad snakes, the grass within the circle, alive with the magic of the place, writhed about their feet, shackling them in a net of blade and root, tight as a vise.

As if in some dark dream, Colin and Susan strained to tear themselves free, but they were held like wasps in honey.

Slowly the figure rose from its seat and came toward them. Of human shape it was, though like no mortal man, for it stood near eight feet high, and was covered from head to foot in a loose habit, dank and green, and ill concealing the terrible thinness and spider strength of the body beneath. A deep cowl hid the face, skin mittens were on the wasted hands, and the air was laden with the reek of foul waters.

The creature stopped in front of Susan and held out a hand: not a word was spoken.

"No!" gasped Susan. "You shan't have it!" And she put her arm behind her back.

"Leave her alone!" yelled Colin. "If you touch her Cadellin will *kill* you!"

The shrouded head turned slowly toward him, and he gazed into the cavern of the hood; courage melted from him, and his knees were water.

Then, suddenly, the figure stretched out its arms and seized both the children by the shoulder.

They had no chance to struggle or to defend themselves. With a speed that choked the cry of anguish in their throats, an icy numbness swept down from the grip of those hands into their bodies, and the children stood paralyzed, unable to move a finger.

In a moment the bracelet was unfastened from Susan's wrist, and the grim shape turned on its heel and strode into the mist. And the mist gathered around it and formed a swirling cloud that moved swiftly away among the trees, and was lost to sight.

The sun shone upon the stone circle, and upon the figures standing motionless in the center. The warm rays poured life and feeling into those wooden bodies, and they began to move. First an arm stirred jerkily, doll-like, then a head turned, a leg moved, and slowly the numbness drained from their limbs, the grass released its hold, and the children crumpled forward onto their hands and knees, shivering and gasping, the blood in their heads pounding like trip-hammers.

"Out—circle!" wheezed Colin.

They staggered sideways and almost fell down a small bank onto a path.

"Find Cadellin: perhaps . . . he . . . can stop it. I think that may be . . . Stormy Point ahead."

Their legs were stiff, and every bone ached, but they hurried along as best they could, and a few minutes later they cried out with relief, for the path did indeed come out on Stormy Point.

Across the waste of stones they ran, and down to the iron gates; and when they came to the rock they flung themselves against it, beating with their fists, and calling the wizard's name. But bruised knuckles were all they achieved: no gates appeared, no cavern opened.

Colin was in a frenzy of desperation. He prized a stone out of the ground, almost as big as his head, and, using both hands, began to pound the silent wall, shouting, "Open up! Open up! Open up! ! Open up! ! Open up! ! !"

"Now that is no way to come a-visiting wizards," said a voice above them.

7

FENODYREE

COLIN AND SUSAN looked up, not knowing what to expect:
the voice sounded friendly, but was that any guide now?

Over the top of the rock dangled a pair of feet, and
between these were two eyes, black as sloes, set in a leathery
face, bearded and bushy-browed.

"Rocks are old, stubborn souls; they were here before
we came, and they will be here when we are gone. They
have all the time there is, and will not be hurried."

With this, the face disappeared, the legs swung out of
sight, there was a slithering noise, a bump, and from behind the rock stepped a man four feet high. He wore a
belted tunic of gray, patterned with green spirals along the
hem, pointed boots, and breeches bound tight with leather
thongs. His black hair reached to his shoulders, and on
his brow was a circlet of gold.

"Are—are you a dwarf?" said Susan.

"That am I." He bowed low. "By name, Fenodyree;
Wineskin or Squabnose, to disrespectful friends. Take your
pick."

He straightened up and looked keenly from one to the other of the children. His face had the same qualities of wisdom, of age without weakness, that they had seen in Cadellin, but here there was more of merriment, and a lighter heart.

"Oh please," said Susan, "take us to the wizard, if you can. Something dreadful has happened, and he must be told at once, in case it's not too late."

"In case what is not too late?" said Fenodyree. "Oh, but there I go, wanting gossip, when all around is turmoil and urgent deeds! Let us find Cadellin."

He ran his hand down the rough stone, like a man stroking the flanks of a favorite horse. The rock stirred ponderously and clove in two, and there were the iron gates, and the blue light of Fundindelve.

"Now the gates," said Fenodyree briskly. "My father made them, and so they hear me, though I have not the power of wizards."

He laid his hand upon the metal, and the gates opened.

"Stay close, lest you lose the way," called Fenodyree over his shoulder.

He set off at a jog trot down the swift-sloping tunnel. Colin and Susan hurried after him, the rock and iron closed behind them, and they were again far from the world of men.

Down they went into the Edge, and came at last, by many zigzag paths, to the cave where they had rested after their first meeting with Cadellin. And there they found him: he had been reading at the table, but had risen at the sound of their approach.

"The day's greeting to you, Cadellin Silverbrow," said Fenodyree.

"And to you, Wineskin. Now what bad news do you bring me, children. I have been expecting it, though I know not what it may be."

"Cadellin," cried Susan, "my Tear must be Firefrost, and it's just been stolen!"

"What—tear is this?"

"*My* Tear! The one my mother gave me. She had it from Bess Mossock."

And out poured the whole story in a tumble of words.

The wizard grew older before their eyes. He sank down upon his chair, his face lined and gray.

"It is the stone. It is the stone. No other has that heart of fire. And it was by me, and I did not hear it call."

He sat, his eyes clouded, a tired, world-weary, old man.

Then wrath kindled in him, and spread like flame. He sprang from his chair with all the vigor of youth, and he seemed to grow in stature, and his presence filled the cave.

"Grimnir!" he cried. "Are you to be my ruin at the end? Quick! We must take him in the open before he gains the lake! I shall slay him, if I must."

"Nay, Cadellin," said Fenodyree. "Hot blood has banished cool thought! It is near an hour since the hooded one strode swampwards; he will be far from the light by now, and even you dare not follow there. He would sit and mock you. Would you want that, old friend?"

"Mock me! Why did he leave these children unharmed, if not for that? It is not his way to show mercy for mercy's sake! And how else could despair have been brought to me so quickly? I am savoring his triumph now, as he meant me to.

"But what you say is reason: for good or ill the stone is with him. All we can do is guard, and wait, though I fear it will be to no good purpose."

He looked at the children, who were standing dejectedly in the middle of the cave.

"Colin, Susan; you have witnessed the writing of a dark chapter in the book of the world, and what deeds it will bring no man can tell: but you must in no way blame yourselves for what has happened. The elf-road would have been but short refuge from him who came against you this day—Grimnir the hooded one."

"But *what* is he?" said Susan, pale with the memory of their meeting.

"He is, or was, a man. Once he studied under the wisest of the wise, and became a great lore-master: but in his lust for knowledge he practiced the forbidden arts, and the black magic ravaged his heart, and made a monster of him. He left the paths of day, and went to live, like Grendel of old, beneath the waters of Llyn-dhu, the Black Lake, growing mighty in evil, second only to the ancient

68

creatures of night that attend their lord in Ragnarok. And it is he, archenemy of mine, who came against you this day."

"No one in memory has seen his face or heard his voice," added Fenodyree. "Dwarf-legend speaks of a great shame that he bears therein; a gadfly of remorse, reminding him of what he is, and of what he might have been. But then that is only an old tale we learned at our mother's knee, and not one for this sad hour."

"Nor have we time for folk-talk," said Cadellin. "We must do what we can, and that quickly. Now tell me, who can have seen the stone and recognized it?"

"Well, nobody . . ." said Colin.

"Selina Place!" cried Susan. "Selina Place! My Tear went all misty! Don't you remember, Colin? She must have seen my Tear and stopped to make certain."

"Ha," laughed Fenodyree bitterly. "Old Shape-shifter up to her tricks! We might have guessed the weight of the matter had we but known *she* was behind it!"

"Oh, why did you not tell me this when we first met?" the wizard shouted.

"I forgot all about it," said Colin: "it didn't seem important. I thought she was queer in the head."

"Important? Queer? Hear him! Why, Selina Place, as she is known to you, is the chief witch of the morth-brood! Worse, she is the Morrigan, the Third Bane of Logris!"

For a moment it seemed as though he would erupt in anger, but, instead, he sighed, and shook his head.

69

"No matter. It is done."

Susan was almost in tears. She could not bear to see the old man so distraught, especially when she felt responsible for his plight.

"Is there nothing we can do?"

The wizard looked up at her, and a tired smile came to his lips.

"Do? My dear, I think there is little any of us can do now. Certainly, there will be no place for children in the struggle to come. It will be hard for you, I know, but you must go from here and forget all you have seen and done. Now that the stone is out of your care you will be safe."

"But," cried Colin, "but you can't mean that! We want to help you!"

"I know you do. But you have no further part in this. High Magic and low cunning will be the weapons of the fray, and the valor of children would be lost in the struggle. You can help me best by freeing me from worry on your behalf."

And, without giving the children further chance to argue, he took them by the hand, and out of the cave. They went in misery, and shortly stood above the swamp on the spot where they had first met the wizard, three nights ago.

"Must we *really* not see you again?" said Colin. He had never felt so wretched.

"Believe me, it must be so. It hurts me, too, to part from

friends, and I can guess what it is to have the door of wonder and enchantment closed to you when you have glimpsed what lies beyond. But it is also a world of danger and shadows, as you have seen, and ere long I fear I must pass into these shadows. I will not take you with me.

"Go back to your own world: you will be safer there. If we should fail, you will suffer no harm, for not in your time will Nastrond come.

"Now go. Fenodyree will keep with you to the road."

So saying, he entered the tunnel. The rock echoed: he was gone.

Colin and Susan stared at the wall. They were very near to tears, and Fenodyree, weighed down with his own troubles, felt pity for them in their despondency.

"Do not think him curt or cruel," he said gently. "He has suffered a defeat that would have crushed a lesser man. He is going now to prepare himself to face death, and worse than death, for the stone's sake; and I and others shall stand by him, though I think we are for the dark. He has said farewell because he knows there may be no more meetings for him this side of Ragnarok."

"But it was all our fault!" said Colin desperately. "We *must* help him!"

"You will help him best by keeping out of danger, as he said; and that means staying well away from us and all we do."

"Is that really the best way?" said Susan.

"It is."

"Then I suppose we'll have to do it. But it will be very hard."

"Is his task easier?" said Fenodyree.

They walked along a path that curved around the hillside, gradually rising till it ran along the crest of the Edge.

"You will be safe now," said Fenodyree, "but if you should have need of me, tell the owls in farmer Mossock's barn: they understand your speech, and will come to me, but remember that they are guardians for the night and fly like drunken elves by day."

"Do you mean to say all those owls were sent by you?" said Colin.

"Aye, my people have ever been masters of bird lore. We treat them as brothers, and they help us where they can. Two nights since they brought word that evil things were closing on you. A bird that seemed no true bird (and scarce made off with its life) brought to the farm a strange presence that filled them with dread, though they could not see its form. I can guess now that it was the hooded one—and here is Castle Rock, from which we can see his lair."

They had come to a flat outcrop that jutted starkly from the crest, so that it seemed almost a straight drop to the plain far below. There was a rough bench resting on stumps of rock, and here they sat. Behind them was a field, and beyond that the road, and the beginning of the steep "front" hill.

"It is as I thought," said Fenodyree. "The black master is in his den. See, yonder is Llyn-dhu, garlanded with mosses and mean dwellings."

Colin and Susan looked where Fenodyree was pointing, and some two or three miles out on the plain they could see the glint of gray water through trees.

"Men thought to drain that land and live there, but the spirit of the place entered them, and their houses were built drab, and desolate, and without cheer; and all around the bog still sprawls, from out the drear lake come soulless thoughts and drift into the hearts of the people, and they are one with their surroundings.

"Ah! But there goes he who can tell us more about the stone."

He pointed to a speck floating high over the plain, and whistled shrilly.

"Hi, Windhover! To me!"

The speck paused, then came swooping through the air like a black falling star, growing larger every second, and, with a hollow beating of wings, landed on Fenodyree's out-stretched arm—a magnificent kestrel, fierce and proud, whose bright eyes glared at the children.

"Strange company for dwarfs, I know," said Fenodyree, "but they have been prey of the morthbrood, and so are older than their years.

"It is of Grimnir that we want news. He went by here: did he seek the lake?"

The kestrel switched its gaze to Fenodyree, and gave a

series of sharp cries, which obviously meant more to the dwarf than they did to the children.

"Aye, it is as I thought," he said when the bird fell silent. "A mist crossed the plain a while since, as fast as a horse can gallop, and sank into Llyn-dhu.

"Ah well, so be it. Now I must away back to Cadellin, for we shall have much to talk over and plans to make. Farewell now, my friends. Yonder is the road: take it. Remember us, though Cadellin forbade you, and wish us well."

"Good-bye."

Colin and Susan were too full to say more; it was an effort to speak, for their throats were tight and dry with anguish. They knew that Cadellin and Fenodyree were not being deliberately unkind in their anxiety to be rid of them, but the feeling of responsibility for what had happened was as much as they could bear.

So it was with heavy hearts that the children turned to the road: nor did they speak or look back until they had reached it. Fenodyree, standing on the seat, legs braced apart, with Windhover at his wrist, was outlined against the sky. His voice came to them through the still air.

"Farewell, my friends!"

They waved to him in return, but could find no words.

He stood there a moment longer before he jumped down and vanished along the path to Fundindelve. And it was as though a veil had been drawn across the children's eyes.

PART 2

8

MIST OVER LLYN-DHU

AUTUMN CAME and in September Colin and Susan started school. Work on the farm kept them busy outside school hours, and it was not often they visited the Edge. Sometimes on the weekend they could go there, but then the woods were peopled with townsfolk who, shouting and crashing through the undergrowth, and littering the ground with food wrappings and empty bottles, completely destroyed the atmosphere of the place. Once, indeed, Colin and Susan came upon a family sprawled in front of the iron gates. Father, his back propped against the rock itself, strained, redder than his suspenders, to lift his voice above the blare of a portable radio to summon his children to tea. They were playing soldiers in the Devil's Grave.

Nothing remained. This place, where beauty and terror had been as opposite sides of the same coin, was now a playground of noise. Its spirit was dead—or hidden. There was nothing to show that svart or wizard had ever existed: nothing, except a barn full of owls at Highmost

Redmanhey, and an empty wrist where once a bracelet had been.

The loss of the bracelet was the cause of slight friction between the Mossocks and the children. Bess was the first to notice that the stone had gone, and Susan, not knowing what to do for the best, poured out the whole story. It was really too much for anyone to digest at once, and Bess could not think what to make of it at all. She was upset over the loss of the Bridestone, naturally, but what troubled her more was the fact that Susan should be so fearful of the consequences that she would invent such a desperate pack of nonsense to explain it all away. Gowther, on the other hand, was by no means so certain that it was all fantasy. He kept his thoughts to himself, but in places the story touched on his recent experiences far too accurately for comfort. However, the affair blew over and no one mentioned it again, though that does not mean to say it was forgotten.

Shortly before Christmas Colin discovered that the owls had left the barn, and for days after, the children were in a fretful state of anxiety over what the disappearance could mean.

"Either Cadellin's got the stone back again," said Colin, "or he's lost the fight."

"Or perhaps it's only that he's sure we're out of danger; or perhaps . . . no that wouldn't make sense . . . oh, I wish we *knew!*"

And although they spent two whole days ranging the

woods from end to end, they found no clue to help them. If there had been a struggle as fierce as Cadellin had predicted, then it had left no trace that they could see.

It was a young winter of cloudless skies. The stars flashed silver in the velvet, frozen nights, and all the short day long the sun betrayed the earth into thinking it was spring. And late one Sunday afternoon at the end of the first week of January, Colin and Susan climbed out of Alderley village, pushing their bicycles before them. They walked slowly, for it was not a hill to be rushed, and the last stretch was the worst—straight and steep, without any respite. But once they were at the top, the going was comparatively good.

They did not ride more than a hundred yards, however, for Colin, who was leading, jammed on his brakes so violently that he half-fell from his bicycle, and Susan nearly piled on top of him.

"Look!" he gasped. "Look over there!"

It could be only Cadellin. He stood against the skyline of Castle Rock, staff in hand, facing the plain.

At once all promises were forgotten: the children dropped their bicycles and ran.

"Cadellin! Cadellin!"

The wizard spun around at the sound of their voices, and made as if to leave the rock. But after three strides he checked his pace, stood for a moment, and then walked to the bench and sat down.

"Oh, Cadellin, we thought something must have happened to you!" cried Susan, sobbing with relief.

"Many things have happened to me, but I do not feel the worse for that!"

There was displeasure in his face, tempered with understanding.

"But we were so worried," said Colin. "When the owls disappeared we wondered if you'd . . . you'd . . ."

"I see!" said Cadellin, breaking into laughter. "No, no, no, you must not look on life so fearfully. We called the birds away because we knew that you were no longer in danger from the morthbrood."

"Well, we thought of that," said Colin, "but we couldn't help thinking of other things, too."

"But what *about* the morthbrood?" said Susan. "Have they still got my Tear?"

"Yes, and no," said the wizard. "And in their greed and deceit lies all our present hope.

"Grimnir has the stone. He should have delivered it to Nastrond, but the morthbrood and he intend to master it alone. Perhaps they believe Firefrost holds power for them. If so, they are mistaken!

"And here we have wheels within wheels; for Grimnir and Shape-shifter, as rumor has it, are planning to reap all benefits for themselves, and to leave the brood and the svarts to whistle for their measure. So says rumor; and I can guess more. I know Grimnir too well to imagine

80

that he would willingly share power with anyone, and the Morrigan, for all her guile, is no match for him. And it may be among all this treachery that we shall find our chance; but for the present we watch, and wait. Firefrost is not in Nastrond's hand, and for that we must be thankful.

"There! You have it all, and now we go our ways once more."

Colin and Susan were so relieved to find the wizard unharmed that parting from him did not seem anything like so bleak an experience as it had been before.

"Is there still nothing we can do?" asked Susan.

"No more than you have been doing all these months. You have played your part well (if we forget this afternoon!), and you must continue to do so, for we do not want you to fall foul of *that* one again."

He pointed with his staff. About the trees through which the Black Lake could normally be seen hung a blanket of fog. Elsewhere, as far as the eye could see, the sunset plain was free of haze or mist, but Llyn-dhu brooded under a fallen cloud.

"It has been there for over a week," said the wizard. "I do not know what he is about, but my guess is that he is trying to seal Firefrost within a circle of magic to prevent its power from reaching Fundindelve. He will not succeed, and he has not the strength to destroy the stone. But then, I have not the power to take it by force, so the matter rests, though we do not."

Cadellin walked with the children as far as the road, and they left him, lighter at heart than they had been for many a day.

The mist was still there the following morning. Colin and Susan had set out on their bicycles soon after dawn to spend the day exploring the countryside, and when they had reached the top of the "front" hill Colin had suggested taking another look at Llyn-dhu. So there they now were, sitting on Castle Rock, and gazing at the mist.

For a long time they were silent, and when next Colin spoke he did no more than put his sister's thoughts into words.

"I wonder," he said, "what it's like . . . close to."

"Do you think we'd be breaking a promise if we went just to look?

"Well, we're *looking* now, and we'd be doing the same thing, only from a lot nearer, wouldn't we?"

That decided it: but then they realized that they had not the least idea of how to reach the lake. However, by picking out what few landmarks they knew, it seemed that if they made for Wilmslow, and there turned left, they would be heading in something like the right direction. So, without further delay, Colin and Susan rode to Alderley, bought a bottle of lemonade to go with their sandwiches, mailed a view of Stormy Point to their father and mother, and within thirty minutes of making their decision were in the center of Wilmslow, and wondering which road to take next.

"There's the man to ask," said Colin.

He had seen a small beetle of a car, from which was emerging a police sergeant of such vast proportions that he hid the car almost completely from view. It was incredible that he could ever have fitted into it, even curled up.

The children cycled over to him, and Colin said:

"Excuse me, can you tell us the way to Llyn-dhu, please?"

"Where?" said the sergeant in obvious surprise.

"Llyn-dhu, the Black Lake. It's not far from here."

The sergeant grinned.

"You're not pulling my leg, are you?"

"No," said Susan, "we're not—promise!"

"Then somebody must be pulling yours, because there's no such place of that name round here that *I* know of, and I've been at Wilmslow all of nine years. Sounds more Welsh than anything."

Colin and Susan were so taken aback that, for a moment, they could not speak.

"But we saw it from Castle Rock less than an hour ago!" said Susan, and tears of exasperation pricked her eyes. "Well we didn't really see it, because it was covered in mist, but we *know* it's there."

"Mist, did you say? Ah, now perhaps we're getting somewhere. There's been fog on Lindow Common for days, and the only lake in the district is there. Do you think that's what you want?"

Llyn-dhu, Lindow: it could be: it *had* to be!

"Ye-es; yes, that's it," said Colin. "We must have got the name wrong. Is it far?"

They followed the sergeant's directions, and after a mile came upon an expanse of damp ground, covered with scrub, and heather, and puddles. A little way off the road was a notice board which stated that this was Lindow Common, and that cycling was prohibited. And in the middle of the common was a long lake of black peat-stained water.

The children stood on the slimy shore. The air was dank, and the scenery depressing. The common was encircled by a broken rash of houses, such as may be seen, like a ring of pink scum, on the outskirts of most of our towns and villages today.

"Garlanded with mosses and mean dwellings." Fenodyree's words came back to the children as they looked at the brick-pocked landscape. But what was most obviously wrong was that they could see all this. For if they were indeed at Llyn-dhu, then, within the space of an hour, it had rid itself of every trace of the mist that had enshrouded it for the last ten days.

"Do you think this is it?" said Colin.

"Ugh, yes! There couldn't be *two* like this, and it's a black lake all right! I wonder what's happened."

"Oh, let's go," said Colin: "this place gives me the willies. We've done what we set out to do; now let's enjoy the rest of the day."

After a cup of coffee in Wilmslow to dispel the Lindow gloom, the children pedaled back toward Alderley. They had no plans, but the sun was warm, and there were a good six hours of daylight left to them.

They were crossing the station bridge at Alderley when they saw it. A light breeze, blowing from the northeast, trailed the village smoke slowly along the sky, but halfway up the nearer slope of the Edge a ball of mist hung as though moored to the trees. And out of the mist rose the chimneys and gaunt gables of St. Mary's Clyffe, the home of Selina Place.

9

ST. MARY'S CLYFFE

THE ROOM was long, with a high ceiling, painted black. Around the walls and about the windows were draped black velvet tapestries. The bare wooden floor was stained a deep red. There was a table on which lay a rod, forked at the end, and a silver plate containing a mound of red powder. On one side of the table was a reading stand, which supported an old vellum book of great size, and on the other stood a brazier of glowing coals. There was no other furniture of any kind.

Grimnir looked on with much bad grace as Shape-shifter moved through the ritual of preparation. He did not like witch magic: it relied too much on clumsy nature spirits and the slow brewing of hate. He preferred the lightning stroke of fear and the dark powers of the mind.

But certainly this crude magic had weight. It piled force on force, like a mounting wave, and overwhelmed its prey with the slow violence of an avalanche. If only it were a quick magic! There could be very little time left now before Nastrond acted on his rising suspicions, and then . . . Grimnir's heart quailed at the thought. Oh, let him but lend this stone's power to his will, and Nastrond should see a true Spirit of Darkness arise; one to whom Ragnarok, and all it contained, would be no more than a ditch of noisome creatures to be bestridden and ignored. But how to master the stone? It had parried all his rapier thrusts, and, at one moment, had come near to destroying him. The sole chance now lay in this morthwoman's witch-craft, and she must be watched; it would not do for the stone to become *her* slave. She trusted him no more than could be expected, but the problem of how to rid himself of her when she had played out her part in his schemes was not of immediate importance. The shadow of Nastrond was growing large in his mind, and in swift success alone could he hope to endure.

With black sand, which she poured from a leather bottle, Shape-shifter traced an intricately patterned circle on the floor. Often she would halt, make a sign in the air with her hand, mutter to herself, curtsy, and resume her pouring. She was dressed in a black robe, tied around with scarlet cord, and on her feet were pointed shoes.

So intent on her work was the Morrigan, and so wrapped in his thoughts was Grimnir, that neither of them saw the two pairs of eyes that inched around the side of the window.

The circle was complete. Shape-shifter went to the table and picked up the rod.

"It is not the hour proper for summoning the aid we need," she said, "but if what you have heard contains even a grain of the truth, then we see that we must act at once, though we could have wished for a more discreet approach on your part." She indicated the gray cloud that pressed against the glass, now empty of watching eyes. "You may well attract unwanted attention."

At that moment, as if in answer to her fears, a distant clamor arose on the far side of the house. It was the eerie baying of hounds.

"Ah, you see! They are restless: there *is* something on the wind. Perhaps it would be wise to let them seek it out; they will soon let us know if it is aught beyond their powers—as well it may be! For if we do not have Ragnarok and Fundindelve upon our heads before the day is out, it will be no thanks to you."

She stumped around the corner of the house to the outbuilding from which the noise came. Selina Place was uneasy, and out of temper. For all his art, what a fool Grimnir could be! And what risks he took! Who, in their senses, would come so obviously on such an errand? Like his magic, he was no match for the weirdstone of Brisingamen. She smiled; yes, it would take the old sorcery to tame *that* one, *and* he knew it, for all his fussing in Llyn-dhu. "All right, all right! We're coming! Don't tear the door down!"

Behind her, two shadows moved out of the mist, slid along the wall, and through the open door.

"Which way now?" whispered Susan.

They were standing in a cramped hall, and there was a

choice of three doors leading from it. One of these was ajar, and seemed to be a cloakroom.

"In here, then we'll see which door she goes through."

Nor did they delay, for the masculine tread of Selina Place came to them out of the mist.

"Now let us do what we can in haste," she said as she rejoined Grimnir. "There may be nothing threatening, but we shall not feel safe until we are master of the stone. Give it to us now."

Grimnir unfastened a pouch at his waist, and from it drew Susan's bracelet. Firefrost hung there, its bright depths hidden beneath a milky veil.

The Morrigan took the bracelet and placed it in the middle of the circle on the floor. She pulled the curtains over the windows and doors, and went to stand by the brazier, whose faint glow could hardly push back the darkness. She took a handful of powder from the silver plate and, sprinkling it over the coals, cried in a loud voice:

"*Demoriel, Carnefiel, Caspiel, Amenadiel! !*"

A flame hissed upwards, filling the room with ruby light. Shape-shifter opened the book and began to read.

"*Vos omnes it ministri odey et destructiones et seratores discorde. . . .*"

"What's she up to?" said Susan.

"I don't know, but it's giving me gooseflesh."

"*. . . eo quod est noce vose coniurase ideo vos conniro et deprecur. . . .*"

"Colin, I . . ."

"Sh! Keep still!"

". . . *et odid fiat mier alve.* . . ."

Shadows began to gather about the folds of velvet tapestry in the farthest corners of the room.

For thirty minutes Colin and Susan were forced to stand in their awkward hiding-place, and it took less than half that time for the last trace of enthusiasm to evaporate. They were where they were as the result of an impulse, an inner urge that had driven them on without thought of danger. But now there was time to think, and inaction is never an aid to courage. They would probably have crept away and tried to find Cadellin, had not a dreadful sound of snuffling, which passed frequently beneath the cloakroom window, made them most unwilling to open the outer door.

And all the while Shape-shifter's chant droned on, rising at intervals to harsh cries of command.

"Come Haborym! Come Haborym! Come Haborym!"

Then it was that the children began to feel the dry heat that was soon to become all but intolerable. It bore down upon them until the blood thumped in their ears, and the room spun sickeningly about their heads.

"Come Orobas! Come Orobas! Come Orobas!"

Was it possible? For the space of three seconds the children heard the clatter of hoofs upon bare boards, and a wild neighing rang high in the roof.

"Come Nambroth! Come Nambroth! Come Nambroth!"

90

A wind gripped the house by the eaves, and tried to pluck it from its sandstone roots. Something rushed by on booming wings. The lost voices of the air called to each other in the empty rooms, and the mist clung fast and did not stir.

"Coniuro et confirmo super vos potentes in nomi fortis, metuendissimi, infandi. . . ."

Just at the moment when Susan thought she must faint, the stifling heat diminished enough to allow them to breathe in comfort: the wind died, and a heavy silence settled on the house.

After minutes of brooding quiet a door opened, and the voice of Selina Place came to the children from outside the cloakroom. She was very much out of breath.

"And . . . *we* say the stone . . . will . . . be safe. Nothing . . . can reach it . . . from . . . outside. Come away . . . this is a dangerous . . . brew. Should it boil over . . . and we . . . near, that . . . would be the end . . . of us. Hurry. The force is growing . . . it is not safe to watch."

Mistrustfully, and with many a backward glance, Grimnir joined her, and they went together through the doorway on the opposite side of the hall, and their footsteps died away.

"Well, how do we get out of *this* mess?" said Colin. "It looks as though we're stuck here until she calls these animals off, and if she's going to do any more of the stuff we've been listening to, I don't think I want to wait that long."

"Colin, we can't go yet! My Tear's in that room, and we'll never have another chance!"

The air was much cooler now, and no sounds, strange or otherwise, could be heard. And Susan felt that insistent tugging at her inmost heart that had brushed aside all promises and prudence when she stared at the mist from the bridge by the station.

"But Sue, didn't you hear old Place say that it wasn't safe to be in there? And if *she's* afraid to stay it must be dangerous."

"I don't care: I've got to try. Are you coming? Because if not, I'm going by myself."

"Oh . . . all right! But we'll wish we'd stayed in here."

They stepped out of the cloakroom and cautiously opened the left-hand door.

The dull light prevented them from seeing much at first, but they could make out the table and the reading desk, and the black pillar in the center of the floor.

"All clear!" whispered Susan.

They tiptoed into the room, closed the door, and stood quite still while their eyes grew accustomed to the light: and then they saw.

The pillar was alive. It climbed from out the circle that Selina Place had so laboriously made, a column of oily smoke; and in the smoke strange shapes moved. Their forms were indistinct, but the children could see enough to wish themselves elsewhere.

Even as they watched the climax came. Faster and faster

92

the pillar whirled, and thicker and thicker the dense fumes grew, and the floor began to tremble, and the children's heads were of a sudden full of mournful voices that reached them out of a great and terrible distance. Flecks of shadow, buzzing like flies, danced out of the tapestries and were sucked into the reeking spiral. And then, without warning, the base of the column turned blue. The buzzing rose to a demented whine—and stopped. The whole swirling mass shuddered as though a brake had been savagely applied, lost momentum, died, and drooped like the ruin of a mighty tree. Silver lightnings ran upwards through the smoke: the column wavered, broke, and collapsed into the ball of fire that rose to engulf it. A voice whimpered close by the children and passed through the doorway behind them. The blue light waned, and in its place lay Firefrost, surrounded by the scattered remnants of Shape-shifter's magic circle.

Colin and Susan stood transfixed. Then slowly, as if afraid that the stone would vanish if she breathed or took her eyes off it, Susan moved forward and picked it up.

In silence she unclasped the bracelet and fastened it about her wrist. She could not believe what she was doing. This moment had haunted her dreams for so many months, and there had been so many bitter awakenings.

In a small room crammed under the eaves Selina Place and Grimnir waited. Both were keyed to an almost unendurable pitch. They knew well the price of failure. Not once in a thousand years had any of their kind disobeyed the charge of Nastrond, but all at some time had stood in the outer halls of Ragnarok and looked on the Abyss. Thus did Nastrond bind evil to his will.

"It cannot be long now," said the Morrigan. "Within five minutes the stone must . . ."

A trail of smoke drifted under the door and floated across the room, and a bubbling sound of tears accompanied it. The Morrigan jumped from her chair: her eyes were wild, and there was sweat on her brow.

"Non licet abire!" She threw her arms wide to bar the way. *"Coniuro et confirmo super . . ."* But the smoke curled around her toward the hearth, and leaped into the chimney mouth. A wind sighed mournfully past the windows, and was still.

"No! No," she mumbled, groping for the door; but Grimnir had already flung it open and was rushing along the corridor to the stairs. He was halfway down the first flight when there was the sound of breaking glass, and the staircase was momentarily in shadow as a dark figure blocked the window at its head. The Morrigan's harsh voice cried out in fear, and Grimnir turned with the speed and menace of a hungry spider.

The noise roused Colin and Susan from their trance. Again the Morrigan shrieked.

"Here, let's get out of this!" said Colin, and he pulled

94

his sister into the hall. "As soon as we're outside run like mad: I'll be right behind you!"

Quite a hullabaloo was breaking out upstairs, and most of the sounds were by no means pleasant: at least they made the other hazard seem less formidable—until Colin opened the door. There was a rasping growl, and out of the mist came a shape that sent the children stumbling backwards into the house, and before they could close the door the hound of the Morrigan crossed the threshold and was revealed in all its malignity.

It was like a bullterrier; except that it stood four feet high at the shoulder, and its ears, unlike the rest of the white body, were covered in coarse red hair. But what set it apart from all others was the fact that, from pointed ears to curling lip, its head and muzzle were blank. There were no eyes.

The beast paused, swinging its wedge-shaped head from side to side, and snuffing wetly with flared nostrils, and when it caught the children's scent it moved toward them as surely as if it had eyes. Colin and Susan dived for the nearest door, and into what was obviously a kitchen, which had nothing to offer them but another door.

"We'll have to risk it," said Susan: "that thing'll be through in a second." She put no trust in the flimsy latch, which was rattling furiously beneath the scrabbling of claws. But as she spoke they heard another sound; footsteps rapidly drawing near to the other door! And then the latch did give way, and the hound was in the room.

95

Colin seized a kitchen chair. "Get behind me," he whispered.

At the sound of his voice the brute froze, but only for an instant: it had found its bearings.

"Can we reach a window?" Colin dared not take his eyes off the hound as it advanced upon them.

"No."

"Is there another way out?"

"No."

He was parrying the lunges and snappings with the chair, but it was heavy, and his arms ached.

"There's a broom cupboard, or something, behind us, and the door's ajar."

"What good will that do?"

"I don't know: but Grimnir may not notice us, or the dog may attack him, or . . . oh, anything's better than this!"

"Is it big enough?"

"It goes up to the ceiling."

"Right: get in."

Susan stepped inside and held the door open for Colin as he backed toward it. The hound was biting at the chair legs and trying to paw them down. Wood crunched and splinters flew, and the chair drooped in Colin's hands, but he was there. He hurled the chair at the snarling head, and fell backwards into the cupboard. Susan had a vision of a red tongue lolling out of a gaping mouth, and of fangs flashing white, inches from her face, before she slammed the door; and, at the same moment, she heard the kitchen door being flung open. Then she fainted.

Or, at least, she *thought* she had fainted. Her stomach turned over, her head reeled, and she seemed to be falling into the bottomless dark. But *had* she fainted? Colin bumped against her in struggling to right himself: she could feel that. And the back of the cupboard was pressing into her. She pinched herself. No, she had not fainted.

Colin and Susan stood rigidly side by side, nerving themselves for the moment when the door would be opened. But the room seemed unnaturally still: not a sound could they hear.

"What's up?" whispered Colin. "It's too quiet out there."

"Shh!"

"I can't see a keyhole anywhere, can you? There should be one somewhere." He bent forward to feel.

"Ouch! !"

Colin let out a yell of surprise and pain, and this time Susan nearly *did* faint.

"Sue! There's no door!"

"Wh-what?"

"No door! It's something that feels like smooth rock going past very quickly, and I've skinned my hand on it. That's why my ears have been popping! We're in a lift!"

Even as he spoke, the floor seemed to press against their

feet, and a chill, damp, air blew upon their faces, and they were aware of a silence so profound that they could hear their hearts beating.

"Where on earth are we?" said Colin.

"It's probably more like where *in* earth are we!"

Susan knelt on the floor of the cupboard and stretched out her hand to where the door had been. Nothing. She reached down, and touched wet rock.

"Well, there's a floor. Let's have our bike lamps out and see what sort of place this is."

They took off their knapsacks and rummaged around among the lemonade and sandwiches.

By the light of the lamps they saw that they were at the mouth of a tunnel that stretched away into the darkness.

"Now what do we do?"

"We can't go back, can we, even if we wanted to?"

"No," said Susan, "but I don't like the look of this."

"Neither do I, but we haven't really much choice; come on."

They shouldered their packs and started off along the tunnel, but seconds later a slight noise brought them whirling around, their hearts in their mouths.

"That's torn it!" said Colin, gazing up at the shaft, into which the cupboard was disappearing. "They'll be onto us in no time now."

10

PLANKSHAFT

THE CHILDREN went as fast as they could, stumbling over the uneven floor, and bruising themselves against the walls. The air was musty, and within a minute they were gasping as though they had run a mile, but on they sped, with two thoughts in their heads—to escape from whatever was following them, and to find Cadellin or Fenodyree. If only this were Fundindelve!

The passage twisted bewilderingly, and when Susan pulled up without notice or warning, Colin could not avoid running into her, and down they sprawled, though they managed to keep hold of their lamps. There was no need to ask questions. The tunnel ended in a shaft that dropped beyond the range of their light. And hanging from a spike driven into the rock was a rope ladder. It was wet, and covered with patches of white mold that glistened pallidly, but it looked as though it would bear the children's weight. The urgency of their plight killed all fear: they dared not hesitate. Both hands were needed for the climb, so they tucked the lamps inside their Windbreakers, and went down in darkness.

The rope was slippery, and it took all their willpower to descend at an even pace. They did this by moving down rung by rung together, Colin setting the pace by counting. "One—two—three—four—five—six—seven." He was ten rungs higher than his sister, and the urge to increase the rate was very strong; he tried not to think of what might happen if Grimnir reached the top of the ladder while they were still on it. "A hundred and forty—and one—two—three—four—five."

"I'm at the bottom!" called Susan. "And it's wet!"

The end of the ladder dangled a few inches above an island of sand that lay at the foot of the shaft, and from here four ways led off, none very inviting. Two were silted up, and two were flooded. Colin chose the shallower of the flooded tunnels, along which stray lumps of rock served as unreliable stepping-stones, and for a few yards the children made dry, if cumbersome, progress. Then Colin, in helping Susan over a particularly wide stretch of water, saw the end of the ladder begin to dance wildly about in the air. Someone obviously had started to descend.

The brown water splashed roof-high as Colin and Susan took to their heels, skidding over slimy, unseen rocks. But the tunnel sloped upwards, and to their relief, they left the water behind and were running on dry sand. This, however, was not long an asset: for soon it lay so thickly that the children were compelled to run bent double, and, finally, to scramble on hands and knees.

What if the roof and floor meet, thought Susan, and we have to go back . . . or wait?

Sweat was blinding her, her hair and clothes were full of sand, stones added to her bruises, and her lungs ached with the strain of drawing air out of the saturated atmosphere: but she had her Tear, and this time Susan was going to keep it, even if all the witches and warlocks that ever were came after her.

Suppose we can't go on, though . . .

But almost at once her fears were allayed: the lamp's beam outlined the end of the tunnel against a blackness beyond.

"Oh, glory be!" she spluttered, and they crawled out onto a soft mound of sand. At first, they could only droop on all fours, heads sagging like winded dogs, and gulp in the cold air, which was a little more wholesome than that of the tunnel; and, from the sudden lack of resonance, they guessed that they must be in a cavern. Every movement in the tunnel had produced a magnified, hollow echo, which made their breathing now appear dry, and remote. The children staggered to their feet, and looked about them.

In shape and size it was just such another cave as the Cave of the Sleepers in Fundindelve, but instead of the light, darkness pressed in from every side. The yellow walls were streaked with browns, blacks, reds, blues, and

101

greens—veins of mineral that traced the turn of wind and wave upon a shore, twenty million years ago.

Colin bent down and listened at the tunnel mouth.

"I can't hear anything," he said, "but we'd better move on, if we can."

Losing their pursuer was an easy task. It seemed that they were in an intricate system of caverns, connected by innumerable tunnels and shafts. These caverns were remarkable. The walls curved upwards to form roofs high as a cathedral, and the distance between the walls was often so great that, at the center of a cave, the children could imagine themselves to be trudging along a sandy beach on a windless and starless night. The loose sand killed all noise of movement, and helped the silence to prey on their nerves: moreover, it made walking hot, laborious work, and the air was still not good; ten minutes under these conditions sapped their energy as much as an hour of normal tramping would have done.

Tunnels entered and left the caves at all angles and levels. They turned, twisted, branched, forked, climbed, dropped, and frequently led nowhere. They would run into a cave at any point between roof and floor, and wind out onto dizzy ledges, which in turn dwindled to random footholds, or nothing at all. And the square-mouthed shafts were a continual hazard. Through some, the distant floors of lower galleries could be glimpsed, while others disappeared into unknowable depths. It was no place for panic. Every corner, every bend, every opening, had to be approached with the greatest caution, for fear of an unwanted meeting; and the caves were the worst of all. After crossing through a half dozen or so, and peering around at the holes which stared sightless from all quarters, Colin and Susan took to scuttling over the floor and diving into the first tunnel they saw, trusting blindly that that particular one would not be tenanted. In the tunnels they were close to wall and ceiling, lamps held their own with shadows; but in the caves the children felt truly lost, for their puny light only accentuated their insignificance, and the feeling of being exposed to unseen eyes grew ever stronger. Somewhere within this labyrinth someone was hunting them down, and Colin and Susan were never more aware of this than when they broke cover beneath a soaring dome of rock and ran through the nightmare sand.

How far they traveled, and for how long before they had to rest, was impossible to judge: time and distance mean little underground. But at last they could go no farther, and, chancing upon a tunnel with a partially blocked entrance, they wriggled inside and lay stretched on the floor. They were consumed by heat and thirst, and fumbled impatiently in Colin's pack for the lemonade. For minutes afterwards the tunnel sounded with gulpings, and gaspings, and sighs of indulgence.

"Better save some for later," said Colin.

"Oh, all right: but I could drink the sea dry!"

The children relaxed their aching limbs, and talked in whispers. But first they switched off the lamps; there was no point in adding to their troubles by hastening the moment when the batteries would be exhausted.

"Listen," said Colin, "the main thing right now is to find a way out of here without being caught. I don't think there's much doubt about where we are; it must be the copper mines. And if that's so, then there are several ways out. But how do we find them?"

They thought for some time in silence: there seemed to be no answer to this problem.

"There must be some . . . wait a minute!" said Susan. "Yes! Look: if we're in the mines the way out must be above us, musn't it? Nearly all the entrances are on top of the Edge."

"Yes. . ."

"Well, if we follow only the tunnels that lead upwards, we're bound to be moving in the right direction, aren't we? I know it's not much of an idea, but it's better than wandering aimlessly until Grimnir and Selina find us."

"It's not only those two I'm worried about," said Colin. "Have you noticed how the sand is churned up everywhere? It's too soft to give clear impressions, but it shows that these mines aren't as empty as they look. And remember what Cadellin said about avoiding them at all costs because of the svarts."

Susan had not thought of that. But the added danger could not alter the situation, and although they talked for some time, they could think of no better plan. Still, it took courage to switch on their lamps and leave their safe retreat for the perils of the open tunnel.

So they journeyed into despair. For no way led upwards for long. Sooner or later the floor would level and begin to drop, and after an hour of this heartbreak Colin and Susan had less than no idea of their whereabouts. Then, imperceptibly, they began to feel that they were gaining ground. They had wormed along the crest of a sandbank that rested on the edge of a cliff, high under the roof of a boulder-strewn cave. Sand rolled continually from under them and slid into the emptiness below: the whole bank seemed to be on the move. At the end of the ridge was a tunnel mouth, and the rock beneath their feet, when finally they made contact with it, was almost as welcome as green fields and the open sky. This tunnel was different: it was longer than most, and less tortuous.

"Colin, this time I think we're on the right track!" said Susan, who was in the lead.

"I think perhaps we are!"

"Oh!"

"What's the matter? Is it a dead end?"

"No, but it's . . ."

Colin peered over his sister's shoulder. "Oh."

The widest shaft they had yet come upon lay before them, and stretched across its gaping mouth was a narrow plank. This was wet, and partly rotten, and no more than three inches rested on the lip of the shaft at either end.

"We'll have to go back," said Colin.

"No: we must cross. The tunnel leads somewhere, or the plank wouldn't be here."

And Susan stepped onto the plank.

Colin watched his sister walk over the pit: he had never known her to be like this before. She had always been content to follow his lead, seldom inclined to take a risk, no matter how slight. Yet now, for the third time in one day, she was deliberately facing great danger, and with a composure that claimed his respect even while it nettled his pride.

Susan was two-thirds of the way across when the plank tilted sideways an inch. Colin felt the sweat cold on his spine: but Susan merely paused to correct her balance, and then she was across.

"There! It's easy—a bit rocky near the middle, but it's quite safe. Walk normally, and don't look down."

"All right! I know how to do it as well as you!"

Colin started out. It was not too bad: the plank was firm, and he was prepared for a slight movement just over halfway. But even so, when it came it caught him unawares. He felt the plank shift: he teetered sideways, his arms flailing. Two swift shambling steps, the plank seemed to swing away from him, the lamplight whirled in an arch, he saw that his next step would miss the plank, the shaft yawned beneath him, and he leaped for his life.

"Are you hurt?"

Colin pulled himself into a sitting position, and rubbed his head.

"No. Thanks, Sue."

He felt sick. For a second, which had seemed an age, he had crouched on one foot, poised over the drop, with his other leg hanging straight down the shaft, unable to produce the momentum to roll forward. And Susan had reached out and grabbed him by the hair, and brought him pitching onto his face in the tunnel.

"Do you mind if we have a rest?"

"We may as well, before we go back over the plank."

"*What?*"

"Look for yourself."

Colin shone his lamp along the tunnel, and groaned. From where they were sitting, the floor plunged down and, for as far as they could see, there was no change in its course.

"Down, down, always down!" cried Susan bitterly. "Are we never going to see daylight again?"

"Let's carry on, now that we're here," said Colin. "You never know, this may be the way out." He did not want to face the plank again, if it could possibly be avoided.

The passage dropped at an alarming rate. The floor was of smooth, red clay, and, once, Susan, going too fast, lost control and slid for several yards before she could stop herself. They learned the lesson and went cautiously from then on.

Down, down, down, farther than they had ever been

before. And then the tunnel veered to the left, zigzagged violently, and came to an end on a ledge overlooking a great void. Colin lay on his stomach and peered over the edge.

"Well, we tried."

Seven or eight feet below was a lake of chocolate-colored water, capped with scuds of yellow foam. Some yards away a bar of sand showed above the surface, but beyond that there was nothing.

"Oh, let's get back to the plank!" said Colin.

All the way up he was wondering how he could bring himself to cross the plank; and there it was before him, and Susan was saying, "Do you think you can manage?"

"Course I can!"

Colin willed himself forward. His ears sang, his legs were rubber, his breath hissed through his teeth, his heart pounded, there was rock under him.

"Nothing to it!"

He shone the light on the plank for Susan to cross.

"Yes, it is easier. It slopes up coming this way." Susan was in the middle now. "I wonder how deep the shaft is." She stopped.

"No, Sue! Don't look down, it'll make you giddy! Come across: don't stop!"

"I'm all right! I want to see how far down it goes." And she turned the beam of her lamp into the shaft. She saw the wet rock, ribbed and gleaming like a gigantic windpipe, fall away beneath her and vanish into darkness far below, and . . . Susan screamed. The lamp dropped from her hand and crashed from wall to wall into the shaft's throat. It was a terrible depth. She swayed, and fell forward, clutching the plank so violently that it began to quiver and grate against its anchorage. Susan knelt, staring into the hole, and whimpering with fear.

"Sue! Sue, get up! What's the matter? *Sue! !*"

"Eyes! Eyes looking at me! Down there in the darkness!"

The plank was trembling alarmingly now, and one corner was almost off the rock. Colin tried to steady it, but he was afraid to pull the plank, in case the other end should be jerked off its support.

"Sue, crawl: don't look down. Come on: it's only a few feet."

"I can't. I'll fall."

"No you won't. Here: look at me: don't look at the shaft. Come on, Sue."

"I can't. I'll fall."

The plank shifted a good inch.

"Sue: look up. *Look up! !* That's better! Now *keep* looking at me, and crawl."

Susan bit her lip, and started to edge her way toward Colin. Immediately the plank began to tremble more than ever.

"I can't do it. Honestly, I *can't!*"

"All right, Sue. Stay there: I'm coming!"

And, without a moment's hesitation, Colin walked out along the plank to join her.

"There now; give me your hand. Do you think you can stand up?"

He bent down, trying to look no farther than his sister's face.

Susan grabbed at the hand, and flung her other arm around his knees: the plank rocked furiously. Colin fought for balance: Susan had completely lost hers. Slowly she pulled herself up, clutching her brother all the time, until she stood, trembling, with her arms on his shoulders.

"Now walk. No, wait: I'll tell you when. With me, now: one . . . two . . ."

Colin moved backwards along the plank, feeling behind him painfully for every step.

11

PRINCE OF THE HULDRAFOLK

"I DON'T KNOW what came over me," said Susan. "I wasn't afraid to begin with: something was pulling me on all the time."

The children had withdrawn a good distance from the shaft, and were sitting with their backs propped against the tunnel wall. They were both in need of a rest.

"I was so certain that we were right that I could have cried when the tunnel dropped like that. And again, when you said we'd better go on, and we came to the ledge, I wanted to jump into the water!"

"That *would* have made a mess of things!"

"I know: but it was such a strong urge. Crossing the plank was easy. I just *knew* it would be safe, and I wasn't dizzy. But, when I saw those four pairs of eyes glowing in the shaft, something went wrong in my head. The plank wasn't safe and wide; it was old, and rotten, and narrow, and the shaft was trying to swallow me, and those eyes were waiting."

"But how do you know they were eyes? It could have

been the light glinting on broken glass, or that white fungus stuff."

"No it wasn't! They blinked, and moved about. I've never been so frightened before; not even when Grimnir caught us. And when I dropped the lamp it was worse.

"But I'm not frightened now: isn't it strange? As soon as we were off the plank I felt altogether different. No, it wasn't because we were safe: it's as though there was a special *kind* of fear reaching out of the shaft and trying to make me fall. Do you think they were svarts down there?"

"I don't know; but whatever they were, I think we'd better move from here. Are you ready?"

They retraced their steps, and presently came to a break in the wall, and a stairway, cut in the rock, leading down into a cave.

"Shall we?"

"Yes, anywhere's better than covering old ground."

But soon they realized that it was not new country at all. They were walking at the foot of a cliff, and on top of this was heaped a shelving bed of sand that almost touched the roof.

"I wish we'd known there was an easier way to that tunnel," said Colin. "It's bad enough down here without doing things the hard way."

They were becoming used to conditions underground, and the atmosphere of the place was no longer oppressive—while they were on the move. But the loss of the lamp slowed them considerably. They went hand in hand wherever possible, and Colin held the light, except when they were in a tunnel: then Susan would take the lead, while Colin was left to grope along behind in treacherous semidarkness. Their rest periods became more frequent, and Colin made a rule of switching off the light at such times. The battery was not new, and they had neither matches nor candles, and without light there would be no hope.

The children tried to keep to uphill paths, but the switchback tunnels bemused them at every turn.

"I'd like something to eat next time we stop," said Susan.

"All right; but we must go very carefully with the food and drink. We were fools to swig nearly all the lemonade like that, because I shouldn't think any of the water down here is fit to drink."

"Ugh, no!"

"The next small tunnel we find, we'll rest and share the food out. We'll have one sandwich each, but we mustn't have any drink."

"Oh, Colin, I'm parched! My mouth feels as though it's full of glue, and I'm so hot!"

"Me too. But we must be strict with ourselves, otherwise we may never get out."

Colin was very worried about the light. It was strong, but sooner or later its white beam would turn yellow, flicker, and slowly die. He said nothing of this to his sister, but she was not blind to the danger.

"Ah, here's a likely place," said Colin.

They crawled inside and looked around. Yes, it was very suitable. The tunnel came to a dead end after a few yards, and the entrance was almost filled with sand. Quite a snug little den—until they realized that it was the very same tunnel in which they had first rested. All that distance, and to no purpose.

"And I was beginning to think we were gaining height!" said Colin. "We're like squirrels in a cage! Oh, I could throw something!"

They unwrapped the food.

"Here you are," said Colin; "make the most of it."

"You know, perhaps we *have* climbed a bit," said Susan. "For all we can tell, this tunnel may be near the surface."

"Huh," said Colin out of the darkness. He knew she was only trying to cheer him up.

Susan gave a little cough, and a gasp.

"What's the matter? Got a crumb in your throat? That's what comes of being greedy! I suppose it means you'll have to have a drink now. Why can't you be more careful?"

Colin reached for the lamp, and pressed the switch. He was alone.

"*Sue! ! !*"

He scrambled around in the tunnel: it was empty.

"*Sue! ! !*"

She had gone, pack and all.

Colin squirmed through the entrance and flashed his lamp up and down: there was nothing to be seen. He ran unthinkingly. Tunnels, caverns, tunnels; a endless desolation of sand and rock.

"*Sue! Sue! !*"

And at once he was past running. The sand dragged his steps, he tripped and fell.

"Sue!" No. That's not the way. Keep quiet. Must think. Put the light out! Must find her. But suppose I find the way out. What then? No. Must find Sue. Rest a minute, though: just a minute.

Slowly strength returned to his limbs. Colin humped himself onto his elbows and turned on the lamp.

Svarts! Two of them. They were creeping over the sand, and were caught full in the beam of light.

Colin sprang to his feet; but he was no longer in danger. To take him in the dark had been their plan; to leap, and grasp him with their sinewy hands, and bear him off in sport. But now they reeled back, their eyes blinded by the lamp. They croaked and hissed, blundering along the cave wall, with their arms before their faces, trying to find refuge from their pain. At length they stumbled upon a tunnel, and fought in haste to enter it. There was a last jostling of leathery backs, and they were gone.

All this happened in half the time it takes to tell, and it was over before Colin could gather his wits: but more was still to come. For a muffled cry sounded along the tunnel, and next the scrabble of feet. A svart burst out of the opening, swerved away from the lamp, and fled across the cave. Hard on his heels was the other svart: he paused, uncertain in the light, looked over his shoulder, and started off after his companion. Something flashed white in the air. The svart shrieked, and crashed on his face in the sand. A broad, two-handed sword had pierced him through and through. Colin's jaw dropped; then, even as his brain struggled to accept the evidence of his eyes, the svart faded, and crumbled like a withered leaf, and all that was left was a haze of dust which settled gently to the floor. For a moment the sword stood reared on its point, then it fell to the ground with a thud.

"Ho! Dyrnwyn, they like not your bite! By the beard of my father, this is poor sport indeed!"

The deep voice boomed out of the tunnel, and into the cave strode a dwarf—a viking in miniature. Yellow hair rolled down his shoulders, his forked beard reached to his waist. His armor was a winged helmet and a shirt of plated mail. About his shoulders hung a cloak of white eagle feathers.

"Breath of Nidhug!" he bellowed, shielding his eyes against the light. "Have I come to this place of unclean air to be half-blinded?"

"I-I'm sorry!" stammered Colin, switching the lamp from the dwarf's face.

"You would have been sorrier ere long, if I had not found you." He took up the sword. "And now come quickly. More svart-heads must roll soon, and I would share them with my cousin."

"But—who are you? And how did you find me?"

116

"Durathror son of Gondemar, am I; Prince of the Huldrafolk, and friend of the lios-alfar. We have not time for gossip: come."

The sword clashed in its sheath, and the dwarf entered the tunnel.

"But wait a minute!" cried Colin. "I've got to find my sister: she's vanished, and I think the svarts have taken her."

"She is safe, never fear. Now will you come, or must I needs carry you?"

Colin had the greatest difficulty in keeping up with the dwarf, for he set off at a run, and slackened his pace for neither steep slopes nor floundering sands. But they had not far to go. Rounding a corner, Durathror slowed to a walk, and there, in a cave from which no other tunnels led, seated on a pile of rocks and calmly eating sandwiches, were Susan and Fenodyree.

"Sue! Where have you been? I thought I'd never see you again!"

"Oh, Colin, thank goodness you're safe, too!" cried Susan. "If it hadn't been for Fenodyree and Durathror I don't know what would have happened."

"I do," said Fenodyree. "And I say it is well we came up with you when we did."

"Came up with us?" said Colin. "I don't understand."

Susan burst out laughing.

"It wasn't Grimnir or Selina Place following us at all: it was these two!"

"*What?* Do you mean . . . ? Oh, no!"

117

"Aye," said Fenodyree, "and a fine chase we had of it!

"But I have heard from Susan of how you gained the stone, and I say Cadellin, old wizard though he is, was wrong to think you have no place in this. You have shown yourselves worthy this day, and I would take you with us beyond the end of adventure, if you so wished it and it should come to that."

"Cousin Wineskin," interrupted Durathror, "well is it said of you that your tongue would still wag if it were cut out. This talk is pleasant, and no doubt there is much more to be said, but our errand is not over, and I would fain rid my lungs of the stink of this place."

"But of course!" said Fenodyree, jumping to his feet. "Forgive me, Durathror. Let us go. The way to the light is not long, and we shall tell all our tales in Fundindelve within the hour."

"I hope so," said Durathror. "But you must know that when I found the Young Dog there were svarts with him, and one, alas, still lives. I feel our journey will be merry ere it is done."

"Quickly then!" said Fenodyree. "We should not have lingered. Susan, behind me: then Colin: Durathror will guard the rear. Nay, do not look so amiss, Colin; Durathror meant no insult. Your name, in my own tongue, is as he said, and it is an old name, and bears much honor. Now let us go with speed."

As they hurried along, Colin managed to find out from

Susan all that had happened to her. It appeared that two svarts had seized her from behind, almost stifling her with their hands, and had carried her off. She had heard Colin's shouts die away, and was on the point of despairing altogether, when there was a loud cry, and the svarts dropped her and ran. She felt someone leap over her and follow in pursuit; but she almost died of shock, she said, when the voice of Fenodyree, close beside her, asked if she was unharmed. In the distance there were two shrieks, followed by the sound of returning footsteps; and so she met Durathror.

"But I don't know how it is they managed to do all this in the dark."

"How can an eagle fly? How can a fish swim?" laughed Fenodyree over his shoulder.

"Yes, but how did you find *me* so quickly?" said Colin. "Was it luck?"

"Luck?" shouted Durathror. "I had but to put my ear to the ground, and your bellowing all but split my head! The wonder of it is that I found no more than two of the svart-alfar in your company."

"Shh!" said Fenodyree, holding up his hand. "We must go carefully now."

He listened, ear to the ground, as Durathror had done.

"Svarts are moving, but they are far away. There may be no danger here, yet."

The tunnel opened into a broad gallery; before them rose

an outcrop of rock, and it was the shape of a lion's head. Above the head the gallery stretched to a great height, cutting through other levels and caves as it went.

"This is the Cave of the Svartmoot, and no place for us at any time."

The words were barely out of Fenodyree's mouth when a faint sound came to them from far away. Colin and Susan had heard it once before: it was the gong that had brought the svart-alfar out of the Devil's Grave on Stormy Point on the night when the children had been run to earth in the marsh below the Holywell.

"Ha!" cried Durathror, and the sword Dyrnwyn sang aloud as she sprang from her sheath in an arc of light.

"Not now: not now," said Fenodyree. "It would be a good fight, but we should go under, and the stone with us. We must pass unseen."

Durathror lowered his arm unwillingly, an expression of disgust on his face.

"By the cow of Orgelmir!" he growled. "Yours is sour counsel! I shall not forget this day. Never before has one of the house of Gondemar turned from battle—and with such carrion, too. When all is safe in Fundindelve I must needs come here and put right this ill."

"Your arm may yet grow tired ere you see the light," said Fenodyree. "That is the call to svartmoot. We must hurry."

He scrambled lightly onto the lion's shoulders, and the others followed. From the shoulder they climbed up a wall,

120

pocked with smooth footholds, to a narrow ledge that curved around to a gallery, overlooking the head. The sound of many feet could now be heard drawing nearer. Every tunnel murmured.

Fenodyree made for a passage that wound into the roof.

"Quickly, now! They are coming by this way, too, and we must reach hiding before they meet us."

The tunnel wall ended, and they were upon a wide platform: far beneath lay the cave. At the back of the ledge was a recess.

"In here! And show no light."

Colin switched off the lamp, and felt the dwarfs press to him as they crowded as far away from the entrance as they could. Susan, crushed against the rear wall, could hardly breathe.

They were none too soon; for barely had they settled themselves when the svarts were upon them. They swept by the opening like a racing tide. For a full minute Colin and Susan listened to the slap of feet, and the hiss of breath. And then the unseen crowd was past, and the noise of its going blended into the general confusion of rustling, croaking, piping, and puling, which grew steadily louder as svarts poured into the cave from every direction, and the air grew rank with their presence.

As though at a given signal, the hubbub died, and a tense quiet fell upon the assembled multitude. The svart-moot had begun.

12

IN THE CAVE OF THE SVARTMOOT

"Do not move," Fenodyree whispered. "Durathror and I go to watch the moot. We shall come back as soon as we know what they intend."

The dwarfs went so quietly that even in that silence Colin and Susan heard nothing.

Below them, some minutes later, a voice began to speak in harsh, high tones. The language was unintelligible; it was full of guttural and nasal sounds, and the words hovered and slurred most jarringly. The speaker was working himself into a state of excitement, or anger, and the crowd was carried with him. It began with a muttering, soon building to a howl at every pause in the address.

Colin felt a hand on his arm.

"Come with me," said Fenodyree. "Shortly you will see; but keep low."

Colin groped his way on all fours till he reached Durathror, who was lying at the edge of the platform, and mumbling into his beard. Not long after, Susan joined them. The noise below was now continuous.

"They are cowards," said Fenodyree, "and must be driven to a frenzy to meet our swords. But he does his work well.

"Ha, I guessed it would be so! They are powerless before a sudden light, therefore they are to prepare themselves with firedrake blood; and here is the Keeper!"

The hysterical voices diminished to a murmur of intense excitement. Then, for a second, the cave was hushed.

"Down!" whispered Fenodyree. "He is taking off the cover!"

A sheet of fire sprang upwards past the ledge, and boiled against the roof.

"Eeee—agh—hooo!" roared the svarts.

The flame sank to a column twenty feet in height, which lit the cave with a red glare. A similar light had burned in St. Mary's Clyffe earlier that day.

"You may look now," said Fenodyree.

Colin and Susan raised their heads, and the memory of what they saw remained with them ever after.

The floor and walls of the cave were covered with svarts. They swarmed like bees. The first two layers of galleries were thick with them, and the children were glad Fenodyree had climbed so high. The lion's head, and a small space beneath its jaws, formed an island in a turbulent sea. On top of the rock stood two svarts, one black, the other white, and they were man-size.

"There you see Arthog and Slinkveal, lords of the svart-alfar. Slinkveal is cunning past the thoughts of men, but Arthog it is who speaks, and carries out his brother's word.

123

See now the firedrake: the eyes of svarts can look on it without pain, and it makes them strong to face the purer light of day: henceforth your lamp will be no weapon."

The flame was rising out of a stone cup, full of a seething liquid, that was held by a hideous, wizened svart who sat cross-legged on the sand beneath the lion's jaws. He was obviously very old, and his sagging skin was piebald, white and black.

"It is time we were gone," said Fenodyree. "We have a comfortless road ahead. Crawl to the tunnel, and do not show your light until I give you word."

For a few yards only, the red glow lit their way. Behind them the tumult increased again.

"There is a corner ahead," said Fenodyree, "and once round that you may use your lamp."

He hurried them along at a relentless pace; and he seemed very despondent. Durathror, on the other hand, was in a much improved temper, and began to laugh to himself as he jogged along behind.

"Did I not say the journey would be merry? Ha! By the blood of Lodur, it is better than all I thought! So we are to be tracked down, are we? And we are to be met at the plankshaft, I hear: and, if all else fails, they wait for us at the gate. Let us hurry to the gate, cousin Squabnose, for I would have these rat-eaters remember the gate in after-time, what few there will be to sing of it when we have passed!"

Fenodyree sighed, and shook his head.

124

"You forget our charge, old Limbhewer. Firefrost is more to us than life, or death in glory: we must sink our pride, and run before these goblins. The gate is not for us."

"Not for us? Then how, pray, shall we gain the upper world? There is no other road."

"There is: just one. And, in its fashion, it bears more perils than the gate, though these cannot be mastered by the sword. At least, if we should perish on this road, Firefrost will lie hidden for untold centuries to come; for we are going where no svart will ever tread, nor any living thing, and only I, in all the world, can tell the way."

"But Fenodyree," cried Susan, "what do you mean? There are lots of entrances!"

"Not here. We are in West Mine, and from it there was one exit made. But so deep did men delve that they touched upon the secret places of the earth, known only to a few; and, of those, my father was the last. There were the first mines of our people dug, ages before Fundindelve: little remains now, save the upper paths, and they are places of dread, even for dwarfs. The way is hidden, but my father taught me well. Never have I trod the paths, save in evil dreams, and I had always hoped to be spared the trial; but now it has come to that."

"Nay, speak this no more," growled Durathror. "I like it not."

They traveled on without rest, talking little, for Colin and Susan had not the energy, and Durathror was subdued by what he had heard.

125

"It is not far," said Fenodyree, "to . . . ah!"

Ahead of them a light flickered on the wall, the source of the light was hidden around a bend in the tunnel, but the dwarfs did not have to guess what to expect.

"What say you now, cousin?" whispered Durathror eagerly. "Do we run like shadows before this light, or do we snuff it out?"

Fenodyree's face was grim.

"We are too near: we must not turn back."

"Good! This shall we do: let the men-children stand here. Go you forward to yonder opening, and stay hidden, with drawn sword, till I call. I shall wait behind this boulder. Hold your ground, Stonemaiden; be not afraid. No svart will touch you, that I can promise!"

And he melted into the dark.

The light grew stronger, and cast shadows on the wall; spindly shadows, with broad heads and hands; and around the bend came the svarts.

There were ten of them, white svarts, with pug-noses. Each carried a torch of wood that had been dipped in the flame of the firedrake's blood. From a girdle around each of their waists hung a crude ax or hammer. The head was a roughly worked stone, kidney or dumbbell shaped; there was a groove about the middle, around which was bent a withy lashed tight with rat-skin thongs.

Colin and Susan involuntarily shrank closer together, and the lamp trembled in Colin's hand. The svarts halted; a

126

deep sigh ran through them; and slowly they began to advance.

In spite of the knowledge that Durathror was close at hand, the children had to fight to stop themselves from running.

The svarts came on: the last of them was past Fenodyree. They held the torches high, and the other hand was poised to clutch. Colin flashed the lamp in their eyes, but they did no more than blink, and laugh hungrily. The children retreated a step. The svarts rushed forward. But at that moment Durathror stepped from behind the boulder, his sword Dyrnwyn in his hand, and bowed low before them, and addressed them in their own tongue.

"Hail, O eaters of toadstools! We are well met!"

The svarts fell back, mouths agape, and hissing after the fashion of giant lizards. But those to the rear of the pack had more courage.

"See!" they cried. "It is he whom we must kill! The men-children are of no matter, but our lords have long wanted *his* life, and for him was the moot held."

"No! No!" screamed another. "There is the maid who tricked us, and see! See! *She has the stone once more! !*"

"The stone! The stone! The stone!"

"The morthbrood have played us false!"

"Or she has stolen it!"

"Seize them! We shall take the stone to ourselves!"

Their eyes glowed green and yellow as desire mastered their cowardice.

127

"Ho!" cried Durathror. "So there is courage in svart-alfa-heim! This is a day of marvels, to be sure! Come, let my sword test the mettle of your new-grown back-bones!"

"We come! We come!"

And they hurled themselves upon the dwarf.

"Gondemar!" bellowed Durathror, and he whirled Dyrnwyn above his head with both hands. Two svarts died under that stroke. They buckled at the knees, and crumbled into dust.

"Gondemar!"

Sparks flew as iron rang on stone, but there were now six svarts in the tunnel, and four torches guttering on the sand. Six to one, far too few for battle, whatever the prize. The svarts turned tail, and ran. Durathror rested on his sword.

"Cousin, it would seem Dyrnwyn is too bitter for their taste: let them then savor Widowmaker!"

Fenodyree came from hiding, and the svarts halted in dismay.

"It is the white one's dog!"

"What does *he* here?"

"It is a trick!"

One of the svarts turned, and ran toward Durathror, but, seeing he was alone in this, he scuttled back to his comrades, who were by this time in distress. Fenodyree was laying about him in silence. He did not feel Durathror's joy of battle: these creatures stood between him and his

128

purpose, and must be killed: that was all. He was no born fighter.

The uproar grew less and less. Fenodyree's round helmet spun under foot, and his mail shirt rang with the dint of blows, but not for long. Soon the two dwarfs stood gazing at each other across a litter of torches and stone hammers.

"I see Widowmaker is well named!" Durathror chuckled. "She has gained two upon me in this fight; I lead you now by one only. I must find me more svarts!"

"Nay, come away, cousin; we must not turn from the path, nor rest, till we are beyond their reach."

Colin stooped to pick up a hammer. It was heavy, but balanced well.

"Shall we take a couple? They may be useful."

"They would drag you to your death, where we are going," said Fenodyree. "Leave them; we do not need such tainted things."

"Durathror," said Susan, as they journeyed on, "where do the svarts go when they disappear?"

"To dust, my Stonemaiden; to dust. They cannot endure the bite of iron: it has a virtue that dissolves their flesh—and would all creatures of Nastrond were as they!"

"Here is the first of our trials," said Fenodyree, "but it is naught that a cool head will not overcome."

Before them the tunnel ended in a drop: they were in the roof of a cave, and across the emptiness another tunnel lay.

A broken ledge, no more than a few inches wide, and sloping outwards, ran to it along the overhanging wall.

"There are handholds," said Fenodyree. "Give me your light, so that you may see, and have both hands free when you come."

It looked so easy as they watched him go crabwise across the wall. He moved smoothly and surely, and in a matter of seconds he was there.

"Susan now, please. If your fingers have need of rest, halfway you will find an iron spike to grip: it is firm. I shall light you."

It was easier than Susan expected, apart from the fact that the lamp could not light hands and feet at the same time, which was occasionally unsettling. Also, she would never have imagined how comforting an iron spike could be. When her hand closed around it, it was as though she had reached an island in a busy street. Susan was loth to leave that spike. She stretched out for the next hold, found it, and was transferring her weight, when something smashed into the wall close by her head, and splinters of rock seared her cheek. She was caught in mid-stride, and for two dreadful seconds she hung by one hand from the spike. The lamp's beam never faltered, and Fenodyree's calm voice checked her panic.

"A foot to the right, Susan. More; more. There. Now draw up your feet; another inch, good. You are safe. Come slowly; do not be afraid."

Across from Fenodyree, Colin had seen the stone ax spin in the lamplight and crash against the rock; and, at the same time, he had heard behind him a sword being drawn.

"Cross as quickly as you may," said Durathror's voice in his ear. "Stay not for me. I go to teach this trollspawn manners."

And, with a ringing cry, Durathror threw himself off the ledge into empty space. As he dropped beyond the light his cloak seemed to fold about him in a curious way.

"Are you ready?" called Fenodyree.

Colin looked across, and saw his sister and Fenodyree together on the other side.

"Yes, I'm ready . . . but Durathror!"

"He knows what he is about. He will not be long."

Nor was he. Colin had just gained the safety of the tunnel mouth when he heard the dwarf's voice right behind him.

"I lead you *now*, cousin! Three skulked below. They heard our coming and hid their torches: they died swiftly."

He was a little breathless, or perhaps indignation had the better of him, for it was the first time he had ever been surprised in ambush.

"But how did you do it?" cried Colin. "I saw you jump off the ledge: weren't you hurt?"

Durathror threw back his head and laughed.

"Woefully!"

He held out his sword hand: the knuckle of his little finger was skinned.

"Do not jest with them," smiled Fenodyree. "They have not long been among us, and there is still much they do not know."

They started along the tunnel. Fenodyree walked very slowly, and when he spoke his voice was grave.

"Listen to me now. We are about to leave West Mine. Were we to stay, we should certainly die, though we took twice four hundred svarts with us, and the weirdstone of Brisingamen would be lost. We may still die: fear is in me greater than I have ever known. I say this now, so that when I lead you into seeming madness you may know that I do not act rashly—or if I do, there is no other course.

"We are to pass through the upper galleries of the Earl-delving to where they touch upon another mine, the like of this, though smaller. The paths were never wide or high, and the earth has stirred many times in her sleep since they were dug: the road may no longer be as I was taught, and we may lose ourselves forever. But it is our only chance, if chance it be, and we must take it. And here is the threshold: once beyond it, we may rest awhile."

They were at the corner of yet another cave. Two of the three walls that they could see were like any other in the mine, rough-hewn and fluted. But the third, immediately to their right, was awesomely different. Its face was smooth and gray, and it shot almost vertically, like a steel spade, into the ground—or, rather, where the ground should have been; for at the dwarf's feet lay a shaft, a sloping chimney of stone. And it was into this that Fenodyree was pointing.

13

"WHERE NO SVART WILL EVER TREAD"

DURATHROR GRUNTED, and picked up a lump of stone and tossed it into the hole. It glanced off the smooth cliff and rocketed out of sight past a bend in the shaft. For an age the hollow crashing of its fall was heard, then silence, and, when all but Fenodyree had judged that that was the end, a single, final, thump.

"We must go down *there?*" whispered Susan.

"And before our courage fails. Durathror, will Valham aid us here?"

"Nay, cousin; the magic is mine alone; and I could not take you, for she was made for elves and finds my un-burdened weight a trial."

"It is as I thought. Will you stay here, then, lest svarts roll boulders on our heads?"

"That I *can* do, and will."

"Good. Colin, Susan, follow me; step where I step; do not hurry. So we shall come safe to the end."

Fenodyree began to climb down the oblique first pitch of the shaft, jamming himself into the angle between the two rock faces. Loose stones rattled down before him, and only the biggest sounded the end of their fall.

"There is room for you both here," he called from the bend; "come singly, Colin first."

Colin lowered himself over the edge into the gully, and worked his way down to within a yard of Fenodyree.

"That is near enough," said the dwarf. "Susan!"

"Yes."

"Stop when you are as close to your brother as he is to me: we must not crowd each other."

"Right."

It was unpleasant to crouch there helplessly while a river of stones bounced off head, shoulders, and knuckles; but Susan was not long about it.

"This is the problem," said Fenodyree when the clatter of debris had faded away. "The shaft is like a bent knee, and we are in the crook, therefore the slope down which we can climb is on the opposite side from us. It is steeper, too. But I think I see a way. Across there, about five feet down, is a ledge. If we jump from here and grasp the ledge we shall be well on our road."

"We shall be if we miss!" said Susan.

"The deed is nothing. It is the thought that breeds fear; and we achieve little by lingering."

And Fenodyree jumped. His fingers snatched for the rock, caught it, and he lay against the sloping wall of the shaft, and did not speak or move. At first the children thought he was unconscious, but they were soon to find for themselves how easy it was to be winded in such a fall.

134

"It is a good hold," said Fenodyree. He eased himself a couple of feet from the ledge, and took up a secure position astride a corner of the shaft.

"Throw me your light."

"But what if you drop it?" said Colin.

"I shall not drop it."

Colin let the lamp fall, and the dwarf caught it in both hands.

"Now jump: you cannot miss."

Can't I? thought Colin.

He had a brief impression of blackness stretching under him, and of the ledge hurtling upwards, before the air was squashed from his lungs by vicious impact with the rock. Blue and red stars exploded in his brain, and a vacuum formed where his lungs should have been; but Fenodyree's steadying hand was in the small of his back, and as his senses cleared, Colin realized that his fingers had closed upon the ledge, and were holding him although he was numb from the elbows down.

When the children and Fenodyree had recovered from the effects of the drop they considered the next stage of their journey. Colin was perched just below Fenodyree, while Susan had pulled herself onto the ledge and was wishing she could spare a hand to massage her aching ribs. It felt as though every bone in her body had been shaken loose by her fall.

"There are no more bends for a distance," said Fenodyree, "but whether there is a safe passage I cannot tell."

The V-shaped gully continued for thirty feet, and they

made good progress. Fenodyree held the lamp, leaving Colin and Susan both hands free; but light was still a problem. For when Fenodyree was above the children, their shadows hid the rock below, causing them to grope blindly for holds; and when he was below, it was difficult for him to shine the light without blinding them. He could, however, direct their feet to holds that he had tested, so they decided on this order of descent.

At the foot of the gully three sides of the shaft opened out like the shoulder of a bottle, leaving the remaining side, the all but sheer rock face, within reach.

"We can't go down there!" said Colin, aghast. "It's as smooth as ice!"

"The eyes of men were ever blind," said Fenodyree. "Can you not see the crevices and the ledges?"

The children peered down the shaft, but still it seemed to them impassable.

"Ah well, you must put your trust in me, that is all. We shall rest here a little, for there will be no haven after this until we near the end."

He called up the shaft, "Is all quiet with you, cousin?"

"Aye, though the chill of this place is beyond belief! It is well I have my cloak! Svarts draw nearer, but they move slowly. I fear they will not come in time."

"Are you ready?" said Fenodyree to the children.

"As ready as we ever shall be, I suppose," said Susan.

"Good. Colin, you are well lodged, so your sister will go first. I shall clear a way for you as far as I can. Have

136

patience, and rest while I am gone, for it will be a hard climb."

Fenodyree let himself down to the full extent of his arms, and scuffed around with his toes until he had found, and cleared, a ledge: then he searched for a lower fingerhold, and in this way slowly began the descent. The wall was not quite as smooth as Colin and Susan had thought, but the accumulated sand of years rendered the many cracks and projections invisible to the children's eyes.

Minutes, or hours, later (for it seemed an eternity in the nothingness of the shaft) the children heard Fenodyree returning. Colin switched on the lamp, and the dwarf's face, lined and gray with effort, came into view.

"All . . . is . . . clear. Or . . . nearly so. We must . . . not . . . delay . . . now."

Colin handed him the lamp, and Fenodyree climbed down to his first station, from which he guided Susan onto the rock face. As soon as she was immediately above him, he descended a little farther, and soon Colin was left alone to his thoughts.

Susan and Fenodyree moved quickly, for the holds were precarious, giving no more than finger and toe room, and often barely that. To remain still for more than a few seconds was to be in serious danger of falling. Yet momentum was hard to check, and Susan more than once came near to losing control of her speed; but, with Fenodyree's help, she achieved a balance between these two fatal extremes.

137

Colin had nothing to do but to avoid cramp and to watch the dwindling oblong of light and his sister's foreshortened silhouette. And as he looked, he gradually became aware of an optical illusion. Being in total darkness himself, he could see nothing of the shaft except the small area lit by the lamp in Fenodyree's hand; and as this drew farther away his sense of perspective and distance was lost, so that he seemed to be looking at a picture floating in space, a moving cameo that shrank but did not recede. He was so fascinated by this phenomenon that he barely noticed the cold, or the strain of being wedged in one unalterable position.

The patch of light contracted until it appeared to be no bigger than a matchbox, and Colin was wondering how deep the shaft could possibly be, when the light was extinguished. But before he had time to be seriously alarmed, he heard Fenodyree's voice shouting up to him, though what the message was he had no idea, for distance and the shaft reduced it to a foggy booming, out of which not a single intelligible word emerged. Still, the tone of the voice held no urgency, so he presumed that Susan was at the bottom and that Fenodyree was on his way up—which, in fact, was what the dwarf had intended him to understand, and Colin had not long to wait before the lamp flashed on a yard below where he was sitting.

"Oh," said Fenodyree, "I am a sight . . . weary . . . of this shaft! Durathror!"

"Aye?"

138

"When we are . . . below . . . I shall . . . call. What . . . of the svarts?"

"They went by another road. More follow."

The shelf on which Susan was resting lay at the foot of the wall. At this point there was a kink in the shaft, like the bend of a drainpipe, and Fenodyree had said that the true bottom of the shaft was not far below.

Susan flexed her fingers, and wriggled her toes. The bulk of the descent had not been too bad, once she had developed a rhythm, and her nerves had settled, but the last fifty feet of the wall were perpendicular, and the strain on her fingers had proved too much, and, on three occasions, only Fenodyree's quick reactions had saved her from coming off the rock.

The sound of the dwarf's voice brought Susan out of her thoughts, and she saw that Colin was beginning the final stretch, the crucial fifty feet. He was lowering himself over the sharp ridge that marked the end of the inclined pitch, and it was punishing him no less than it had his sister: he would carry the bruises for days. And how Fenodyree climbed with only one free hand was a marvel. He was nearing the end of his third trip up and down the shaft, and there he was, taking Colin's weight on his shoulder and guiding him to the next hold.

"Twenty feet more, Colin, and we shall be there! Bring your left hand down to the inside of your right knee. Your other hand will fit there, too. Steady! Now lower yourself as far as your arms will let you. There is room for your left foot. Right hand out at your shoulder's level; not so far! There. Six inches down with your right foot." Fenodyree stepped onto the shelf. "Now your left hand to the side of your hip. . . ."

A minute later Colin was standing beside Susan.

"We are not yet at the foot," the dwarf reminded them. "See what awaits."

He guided them down the shelf to the mouth of the lower end of the shaft. The shelf grew rapidly steeper, and very smooth. There were no holds at all.

"What do we do now?" cried Susan.

"We slide! Oh, never fear, it is no great way, and there is sand to break your fall."

The children remained apprehensive, but Fenodyree insisted that there was no danger, and, to prove his word, he sat at the top of the shelf and pushed off with his hands. There was a swish, silence, and a soft bump.

"It is as I said," called Fenodyree, and he shone the light upwards.

"All right," said Susan, "but . . . oh! !"

The chute was far smoother than Susan had anticipated and, caught off her guard, she tobogganed helplessly into the air, and landed at the dwarf's feet with her knees in her stomach, winded for the second time in the space of an hour. It was small consolation that Colin fared no better. Fenodyree had not lied: there *was* sand, but it was wet and, consequently, hard.

While the children lay croaking, Fenodyree cupped his hands to his mouth and shouted:

"Du-rath-ror!"

An answering voice echoed in the shaft.

"We shall rest here," said Fenodyree, "but we must not stay long, for if we do not win clear of the Earldelving by sunset we shall have no choice but to stay there until the dawn, and that would be grim indeed."

"Nay, then," said Durathror, "let us forgo our rest!"

He was standing on the shelf at the foot of the great wall.

"But . . ."

"But how have you . . . ?"

"I fell!" shouted Durathror merrily. "See!"

And he leaped down to join the children and Fenodyree. His cloak swirled about him, and he landed lightly on his feet with as little disturbance as if he had skipped from the bottom treads of a staircase.

The foot of the shaft opened into a small chamber, three or four feet high, and it was flooded except for the pyramid of sand in the middle.

Fenodyree bade the others make themselves as comfortable as possible, but it was not easy to stay dry, and, at the same time, to be out of the path of any svart-sent boulders that might land in their midst.

Colin and Susan divided the remains of the food and drink among the four of them. And as they ate, the dwarfs pieced together the events that had brought them so unexpectedly to hand in time to rescue Susan and to bring havoc among the svarts.

This was their story. Durathror and Fenodyree were walking near Castle Rock when the kestrel Windhover brought news that Grimnir had risen from the lake and had entered St. Mary's Clyffe. The dwarfs knew that where Grimnir was, there would be Firefrost, and that this might be their chance. Cadellin was prowling in the hills toward Ragnarok to find out if word of the stone had spread, for he was as anxious as Grimnir to keep its present whereabouts a secret. He could not possibly come; so the dwarfs decided to attack alone, and in no time Fenodyree had gathered his armor, and they were on their way.

They heard of the children's arrival from Windhover, whom they had arranged to meet in the cover of the garden next to St. Mary's Clyffe. Grimnir and the Morrigan, said Windhover, were in an upper room: there was unpleasantness behind curtains downstairs. The hounds were loose.

"Do you wait by the entrance wall," said Durathror.

"Windhover shall take me where these morthdoers hide, and I shall disturb them, and, with Dyrnwyn, drive all thought of Firefrost from their heads. Wait for a space after you hear me fall upon them, seek the stone in the lower room, for there I think it will be, and so to Fundindelve, where I shall join you if I may."

Then Durathror went with the kestrel to the room under the eaves. It was as Colin and Susan had begun to suspect; he had the power of flight. It lay in his cloak of eagle feathers, a survival from the elder days, and a token of great friendship.

When his moment came, Fenodyree ran for the door: to his surprise it was open, and he entered warily. On finding the curtained room empty he was perplexed, but he had no time to search farther, for as he was about to try the kitchen door it was thrown open, and Durathror cannoned into him. There was savage joy stamped on his face as he spun Fenodyree into the cloakroom where the children had lately been hiding, and closed the door. Seconds later Grimnir stumbled out of the kitchen, followed by Shape-shifter. The empty room, the open door.

"The dwarf has taken it!" screamed Shape-shifter, and they both rushed out into the mist.

"Have you the stone?" whispered Fenodyree incredulously.

"Nay, but it is in good hands!"

They came out from the cloakroom: the mist had rolled away: in the distance a hound bayed.

"I could not kill the morthdoers, since their magic is greater than my sword, but they will feel her smarts for many a day." Durathror chuckled. "I came to join you in the end, but, entering yonder room, I saw two things to make me pause. There is a cupboard against the wall, and a hound of the Morrigan made clamor against it; but the door was closed, and I had seen what closed it—a small white hand, cousin, and Firefrost shone upon the wrist! I slew the beast: the rest you know."

Fenodyree ran into the kitchen.

"Come out, children! Susan! Colin!" He seized the cupboard handle. "Oh, you will be remembered when . . ." He stared into the shaft, and saw a square of wood begin to grow rapidly larger as it climbed toward him out of the far depths.

"And it was but luck that brought us to you when we were beyond hope," said Durathror.

"If only we'd known!" cried Susan.

"Aye," said Fenodyree; " 'if only.' We should have been in Fundindelve ere now."

The children told their story, and when they described the crossing of the plank the dwarfs grew very excited.

"Hair of the Moondog!" shouted Durathror. "And did you not go on?"

"Oh yes," said Colin, "but the tunnel finished on a platform over a lake."

Durathror put both hands to his head and groaned in mock despair.

"Had you but known it," said Fenodyree sadly, "the water is little more than a foot deep, and the way from there leads to the gate, not half a mile distant."

After such a revelation the children had not the heart to talk. They huddled, wrapped in their thoughts, and their thoughts were the same. Here they sat, at the bottom of a shaft, at the end of the world: they had gained the weirdstone of Brisingamen, but that success promised to be

144

the beginning, and not the end, of danger, and where it would lead them they dared not think.

"We must move now," said Fenodyree.

When they switched on the light Colin and Susan examined their surroundings in detail for the first time: and an awful truth dawned on them. There was no obvious way out of the chamber. Two tunnels led off in opposite directions, but they were flooded, and the roofs dropped steadily to meet the green-tinged water.

"Fenodyree! How do we get out of here?"

"Aye, cousin," said Durathror, "all the while since I came I have sought a way to leave, but I see none."

Fenodyree nodded toward the smaller of the tunnels.

"Did I not say that the road was hard? Colin, is the wrapping for your food proof against water?"

"Yes, I think so. But Fen . . . ! !"

"Then when we start, cover the light with it. You will have to trust to my eyes alone for a time."

"And may I have your covering for Valham, my cloak?" said Durathror to Susan.

He unbuckled his feathered cloak and rolled it tightly to fit into the sandwich bag, and Susan fastened it in her pack, which if anything, seemed lighter for the load.

"Put out the light," said Fenodyree. "And have courage."

14

THE EARLDELVING

THE WATER was so cold that it took their breath away. Even Durathror, the hardened warrior, could not stifle the cry that broke from his lips at the first shock.

They waded along the tunnel for a short distance before having to swim, and they had not gone much farther when Fenodyree stopped and told the others to wait while he went ahead. He drew a deep breath, there was a flurry and a splash, and he did not answer when Colin spoke.

"Where has he gone?" asked Susan.

"The roof and water meet where he left us," said Durathror.

Two minutes passed before Fenodyree broke the surface again, and it was some time after that before he could speak.

"It is no distance," he said when at length his breathing was under control, "and the air is fresh, but the roof is low for many yards, so we must swim on our backs."

Another swirl, and he was gone.

"I'll wait about a minute," said Susan. She was more frightened than she cared to admit, but she hoped Colin and Durathror would think that her teeth were chattering with the cold alone.

"Right: here goes."

"She has great courage," said Durathror. "She hides her fear better than any of us."

"Are you scared, too?" said Colin.

"Mortally. I will pit my wits and sword against all odds, and take joy in it. But that is not courage. Courage is fear mastered, and in battle I am not afraid. Here, though, the enemy has no guile to be countered, no substance to be cast down. Victory or defeat mean nothing to it. Whether we win or lose affects us alone. It challenges us by its presence, and the real conflict is fought within ourselves. And so I am afraid, and I know not courage."

"Oh," said Colin. He felt less isolated now, less shut in with his fears. "Well, I'd better be on my way."

"Good luck to you," said Durathror.

Colin held his dive as long as possible, but the icy water constricted his lungs, and he soon was in need of air. He rose to what he implored would be the surface, but his hands and the back of his head scraped against the roof. Flustered, he kicked himself into a shallow dive, his stomach tightening, and his head seeming about to burst. This time. No! Again he struck the roof. What was wrong? Why was there no air? Fenodyree had said . . . ah! He remembered! Swim on your back: the roof is low. That's it! Colin turned frantically onto his back: the knapsack pulled at his shoulders and began to tilt him upside down.

147

He threshed the water and managed to right himself. And then his lips broke surface. The air rushed out of his lungs, and Colin promptly sank, swallowing a lot of water. He kicked off so violently from the tunnel floor that he nearly stunned himself on the roof, but it quelled the panic, and he lay on his back, breathing air and water by turns.

The roof was certainly low. In order to keep his lips above water he had to squash his nose against the rough stone of the ceiling, which made progress as painful as it was difficult.

After twenty yards, Colin was relieved to find that the distance between surface and roof was increasing, and, before long, he was able to turn onto his face and swim more naturally. But where were the others? He trod water.

"Hello! Ahoy! Sue!"

"Here!"

It was Susan's voice, and not far ahead, either. Almost at once the water grew shallow, and then he was knee-deep in mud, and Fenodyree's arm was about him.

"Oh, let me sit down!"

Durathror joined them presently, and he was in great distress.

"Squabnose," he gasped, "I have been near death many times, but never has he stretched out his hand so close, or looked more terrible!"

Colin unwrapped the lamp to discover how it had withstood the rough passage. It was none the worse, and by its light the children saw that they were lying on a bank of red mud, soft and very sticky. Ahead of them was a tunnel, but it was far different from any in West Mine. The roof ran square to the walls, and nowhere was more than a yard high. The colors were striking, for the walls were of a deep-red shale, and the roof was a bed of emerald copper ore.

The going was difficult enough without the mud. It was not so bad for the dwarfs, but Colin and Susan developed a severe ache in neck and back very quickly. The tunnels never ran straight, and they would branch five times in as many yards. Caves were few, and seldom bigger than an average room. Water was everywhere; and what few shafts barred the way were flooded, and therefore easily crossed.

After half a mile the relatively open passages were left behind, and now even the dwarfs were forced to crawl all the time. Roof falls became frequent too, and negotiating them was an arduous business. The children were continually surprised by the way in which it was possible to force their bodies through holes and cracks that looked as though they would have been a squeeze for a kitten, but they found that, no matter how impracticable a gap appeared, if a head and one arm could be pushed through together, then the rest of the body would, eventually, follow.

Now and again they would come upon a stretch of rock over which the water had washed a delicate curtain. This was to be found where a vein of ore lay just above the roof: the water, trickling through the copper, over the

149

years had spread a film of color down the wall, ranging from the palest turquoise to the deepest sea-green.

The tunnels grew more constricted and involved. Susan particularly disliked having to worm herself around two corners at once. She thought of the picture of Alice in the White Rabbit's house, with an arm out of the window, and one foot up the chimney.

"That's just how it is here," she grumbled; "only this ceiling's lower!"

Fenodyree called a halt in a cave into which they fitted like the segments of an orange. But they could stand partially upright, which was some relief.

"We have put the greatest distance behind us," said Fenodyree, "but it is from here that our chief dangers lie. Between Durathror's feet is the passage that will take us to the light."

"*What?*" cried Susan. "But that's only a rabbit-hole!"

"If it were the eye of a needle, we should still have to pass through it to gain the upper world. But do not despair: we are not the first to come this way, though I think we shall be the last. My father traveled the Earldelving seven times, and he was an ample dwarf by our reckoning.

"Now we must make ready. Take note of what I say, for this is the last chance of speech until we come to safety, and there will be no room for error."

Under Fenodyree's instructions, Colin and Susan took off their knapsacks—a complicated maneuver in that space —and fastened them by the strap to one ankle. Susan's pack held Durathror's cloak, and Colin was still carrying the lemonade bottle: this he discarded. Fenodyree advised him to put away his lamp, for, he said, hands would be needed more than eyes.

He bade Durathror take off his sword.

"Keep her ever before you," he said, "and so neither Dyrnwyn nor the son of Gondemar will be lost."

And he unbuckled his own sword and pushed it into the opening.

Durathror stood alone in the silence of the underworld. He took the empty bottle that Colin had thrown down, and set it upright in the middle of the floor. A wry smile touched his lips as he looked at it. And shortly afterwards the cave was empty, save for this one monument to wild endeavor.

Both the children had the greatest difficulty in entering the tunnel. For the first yard or so it sloped downwards, and then turned uphill, not sharply, but enough to cause acute discomfort at the bend. Sand choked the entrance, though even when that was behind them the tunnel was so heavily silted that it was almost beyond the children to move at all. They lay full length, walls, floor, and roof fitting them like a second skin. Their heads were turned to one side, for in any other position the roof pressed their mouths into the sand and they could not breathe. The only way to advance was to pull with the fingertips and to push with the toes, since it was impossible to flex their legs at all, and any bending of the elbows threatened to jam the arms helplessly under the body.

The tunnel was unlike any they had met in the Earl-delving, for, although it was not straight, it did not branch. This factor, and the plugging of the tunnel by four bodies, meant that the leader was the only one to be able to breathe at all well.

They became unbearably hot. Sand lodged in every fold of skin, and worked into mouth, nose, and ears.

Colin found that he had to rest more and more frequently. He thought of the hundreds of feet of rock above and of the miles of rock below, and of himself wedged into a nine-inch gap between.

"I'm a living fossil! Suppose I stick here: *that'll* make archaeologists sit up!"

Ahead, Fenodyree was battling with a fresh difficulty. He had reached a spot where the tunnel bent abruptly under upon itself like a hairpin, and teasing Widowmaker's rigid blade through the angle, at arm's length, was no simple task. Strained nerves and muscles are not an aid to fine judgment. He succeeded, but it was some time before he was in any condition to follow his sword. Fenodyree was coming to the end of his last reserve of strength.

Susan felt the obstacle with dismay. It was not possible! But where was Fenodyree? He must have found a way around, so perhaps, like most hazards underground, it was easier than it looked. Anyway, lying there thinking about it would not do much good, so she tucked in her head, and jack-knifed around into the lower level. It was unpleasant, especially when her heels scraped the roof, but her weight carried her down, and it was soon over.

Colin was an inch taller than his sister, and that was disastrous. His heels jammed against the roof: he could move neither up nor down and the rock lip dug into his shins until he cried out with the pain. But he could not move.

Durathror, coming up behind, took in the situation at once.

"Can you hear?" he shouted at Colin's ankles.

"Yes."

The reply was barely audible.

"Try–to–turn–to–your–side! Thence–to–your–belly! I –shall–guide–your–feet! Are–you–ready?"

"Yes."

Durathror's sword jutted beside Colin's feet, and although it was in its scabbard, matters would not be improved if it became entangled with Colin's wildly jerking legs.

Colin wriggled himself around in the tunnel. It was really not possible, but desperation tipped the scales; and once he was on his stomach, his knees bending with the tunnel, there was just enough play for Durathror to force Colin's legs around the angle, and from then on Colin was better off than any of the others, because they were now lying on their backs, and in that position movement was even more exhausting and unpleasant.

Fenodyree jerked his way along with renewed vigor, for this bend was the last great hazard, according to his lore. Imagine, then, his horror when his sword splashed in water. He twisted his head all ways. He could not see; but his hands brought him bad news. The tunnel dipped, and was flooded to the roof. This had not been so in his father's time: so much for the elder days!

The end of the tunnel was not yet. How far did the water lie? Inches? Yards? He would have to squirm along, holding his breath (and he was panting uncontrollably at the start!), in the hope that he would come to air. Retreat would be impossible, as it was now. And that decided him. Better a quick road to forgetfulness than a lingering one. But it called for nerves of steel to edge forward into the water, and, at the last, under.

This moment was to be endured three times more as Susan, Colin, and Durathror made the choice that was no choice. But once they grappled with the terror it did not last: for the water had collected in a shallow, U-shaped bend, not two yards long, and they all emerged on the other side before their lungs were drained of air. They cried or laughed, each according to his nature, but the sound in all cases was the same.

Not much later the floor began to drop away from the roof, and it was possible to crawl on hands and knees. The children wrestled with the sodden webbing of their packs and talked rapidly and loudly of the perils they had faced, and said how good it was to move freely again.

"Taken all in all," said Fenodyree, "the Earldelving has not used us ill: I had feared it would be more cruel. From here we shall be in little danger, provided that we respect the smaller risks."

They now pressed on with all speed, for there could be scarcely an hour of daylight left, and the prospect of having to spend the night in wet clothes, with mud for a bed, was in no way appealing.

After a time, Susan thought she saw a faint gray blur ahead of them past Fenodyree's shoulder. She switched off the lamp.

"Here, Sue! What are you playing at?"

"Look! Daylight!"

It was: and soon they had reached it. They were at the end of the tunnel, and at the bottom of a shaft. The converging lines of its gleaming, wet sides mounted to a tiny square of blue, a whole world away.

"We've not got to climb up this shaft, have we?" said Colin.

"Nay," laughed Fenodyree, "we shall be in dire straits ere I ask *that* of you! Our way is easier by far."

He raked about with his feet behind the pile of rubbish at the bottom of the shaft.

"It is somewhere . . . ah, I have it!"

He dragged to one side a mass of decaying branches to reveal a hole in the floor.

"Here is the exit from the Earldelving: once through here, we cannot return."

It was a sloping continuation of the shaft, though only half its breadth, and it was cut through stiff clay that glistened without ledge or fissure.

"It is a pleasant ride," said Fenodyree, seating himself on the edge, and grinning at Susan. He peered down between his feet, nodded, and let go. A faint splash marked the end of his glissade, and his voice sounded cheerily a long way below.

Susan lowered herself into the hole with extreme caution, but the edge crumbled beneath her hand, and yet again she disappeared from view like a bullet from a gun. She careered over the greasy surface, faster and faster, and landed waist-deep in a mixture of water and mud that broke her fall, but had little else to recommend it.

"Oh!"

"If you put your hand out to your left," said Fenodyree close beside her, "you will find a corner of rock: pull yourself out with that. Good. Now feel your way round to the tunnel. We shall soon be out of here."

The tunnel was flooded to a depth of three feet, and was sticky with clay, but it was high, and not long. At its end rose a shaft that offered few difficulties, for it was composed of a series of inclined pitches, connected by wide shelves, so that it was more like scrambling up a giant stairway than climbing a shaft. Only the last dozen feet were at all dangerous: here the rock was vertical, but the holds were many, and the top was gained without trouble. From there a short passage led into a circular cave—and daylight; real, accessible daylight. A tree trunk resting against the wall took Fenodyree, with the others packed behind him, up into a gully that overlooked the cave: the gully became a ravine and above was open sky; cold, crisp, dry air filled their lungs.

The side of the ravine was scored with holes and ledges, and children and dwarfs almost fell over each other as they swarmed up the last monotony of stone, out of the eternal, stagnant silences, into light, and life, and wide horizons. Then there was grass beneath them, and a wind upon their cheeks.

15

A STROMKARL SINGS

BEYOND THE RAVINE wound the elf-road, and the dwarfs lost no time in hustling Colin and Susan onto it, but once there they permitted themselves to relax, for as long as they remained on the road, said Durathror, they would be hidden from searching eyes.

They made a bizarre picture in their all-over coats of red mud, encrusted with yellow sand that spared only their more pliable features, and these were daubed with red, as if they were in war paint. But none of that mattered now as they stepped out for Fundindelve, and their aching limbs only sweetened the prospect of rest. After all they had undergone in the barren caves, this scene of beauty, the waning light among the scented pines, was almost unreal.

"It's like a dream," said Susan; "just like a dream. I can even imagine there's music all around us!"

"So can I!" said Colin. "It's like a harp. What can it be?"

"A harp," said Fenodyree, smiling. "See, on Goldenstone, a stromkarl plays."

They had come to a junction in the path, and to their right stood a boulder, with nothing golden about it that the children could see: it was like any outcrop of weathered, gray sandstone, except that it had been crudely worked to an oblong shape by men long dead, and few now can tell its purpose.

On top of the stone sat a young man, plucking the strings of a harp. He was less than three feet high; his skin lustrous as a pearl; his hair rippling to his waist in green sea-waves. And the sad melody ran beneath his fingers like water over pebbles.

> *When summer in winter shall come*
> *Then shall be danger of war.*
> *A crow shall sit at the top of a headless cross,*
> *And drink of the noble's gentle blood so free.*
> *Between nine and thirteen all sorrow shall be done.*
> *A wolf from the east shall right eagerly come*
> *To a hill within the forest height.*
> *Beside a headless cross of stone,*
> *There shall the eagle die.*

"Why do you sing the old prophecies?" said Durathror. "Are they now to be fulfilled?"

"Who knows? I do but sing of the summer that has come in winter. Does your road lead to Fundindelve?"

All the while the stromkarl was speaking, his hands plucked the silver strings, and the tone of his bell-like voice against the background of music was a song. He looked at neither the children nor the dwarfs once the whole time, but concentrated on his harp, or gazed out toward the hills.

"It does indeed," said Fenodyree, "and we take with us the weirdstone of Brisingamen!"

"I am glad," said the stromkarl. "But you will not go to Fundindelve."

"What do you say? How shall we not?"

"The hooded one sits by Holywell, and Shape-shifter watches the gates: and to them are gathering the morthbrood. The svart-alfar will be there at sunset, and with the night are coming others. No birds will fly, save the eyes of the Morrigan. It will be dark within the hour; see to it that you are not under the sky at that time."

"Our swords will be ever at your command for this!" said Durathror. "You have done more than guard our lives."

The stromkarl bowed his head.

"My people will aid you where they may: fare you well!"

And he jumped down on the other side of Goldenstone, and they did not see him again.

"It never crossed my mind that this would be their course," said Fenodyree, "obvious though it was. Oh, I am not wise in judgment as a dwarf should be!"

"Nay," said Durathror, "your wits have served us nobly this day. But what is there for us now?"

160

"I do not know."

"Can we get to the farm before dark?" said Colin.

"That is a *good* plan!" Fenodyree smote his hands together. "With luck, the morthbrood will not hear of your part in this until the svart-alfar come, and they may be late if they are still searching for us in West Mine. We should reach the farm, but whether it will be shelter for the night I cannot be certain."

"What of the stone?" said Durathror.

"We must find Cadellin," said Fenodyree. "In his hands it will be secure, and he can wield its might for our safe-keeping."

"Why, then, give me the stone! He shall have it ere you can reach the farm!"

"Do you see those?" said Fenodyree, pointing across the fields.

"I see; but what of it? Rooks flock homeward daily at this hour, and in greater numbers than are flying there."

"Did you not hear the stromkarl say that no bird flies this day? Those are not rooks: you would be torn asunder within the minute. They know where Cadellin is as well as I, and that we must find him."

"Then how shall we do this?"

"We must go stealthily, on foot, and seek him in the hills."

Colin looked at the rolling mass of the Pennines, out of which the first shadows of night were creeping.

"But how do we find him up there, and how can we move without being seen? It's nearly all open moorland."

"We move by day, when their eyes are weakest, and if there is scant cover for us, there is more chance that we shall see the morthbrood from afar. As for Cadellin, I am to meet him on the summit of Shuttlingslow yonder at dawn on the morning of the fourth day from this. There is little hope of finding him sooner. Our greatest task will be to avoid the morthbrood for so long."

They headed for the farm with all speed, keeping under cover wherever possible, though the lanes were almost deserted at that time of day. Only the occasional farm laborer bicycling home disturbed their progress, for the dwarfs insisted on hiding at any sign of life. "The morthbrood travel in many guises," said Durathror.

They came over the Riddings as the first stars were shining, and they saw Gowther's stolid figure, Scamp at his heels, going the round of the sheds and stables to fasten up for the night. The individual, isolated sounds of twilight, the clink of a chain, the rattle of a door, the ring of boots on cobbles, carried far on the evening air.

Gowther was crossing to the house as the weary party entered the farmyard.

"Hello!" he said, eyeing them up and down. "What have we got here? You look as if you've been through every marl-pit between here and Wornish Nook! Hey, and wheer are your bikes?"

162

"It is a good story, farmer Mossock," said Fenodyree, "but I would fain have a roof over my head for the telling of it."

"What?" said Gowther. He peered hard at the dwarf. "Here, wait a minute, I know thee! You're the feller as threatened me some months back, anner you? Well, I've got a bone or two to pick with thee; *and* I'd like to know what mischief you've been getting these childer into!"

He loomed over the dwarf, and made to grab hold of him, but Widowmaker came from her scabbard like lightning, and the broad blade's point rested against Gowther's cask of a chest.

"I am he: and much sorrow has come of your words that day, though it is not of my doing.

"I mean you no harm, farmer Mossock, and I crave your help; but every moment we stand here exposed to watching eyes adds to our peril. Let us right our grievances behind locked doors."

"You've *got* to trust him, Gowther!"

"You *must!*" cried Susan. "He's saved our lives more than once today!"

"And it *is* dangerous to be out here!"

"You'll understand when we tell you!"

Gowther looked at the anguished faces of the children, then down at the steady blade.

"All reet," he said slowly. "You con come in. But you dunner move a step towards the door while you've got that thing in your *bond*. And think on, I want an explanation; and it had best be good!"

Fenodyree sheathed his sword, and smiled.

"It will be *interesting*, farmer Mossock."

"Well! This is the rummest do *I've* come across! It is that! What about thee, Bess?"

Bess was ironing Fenodyree's rapidly washed tunic, and she pointed with her flat-iron at the two dwarfs, who were squatting on either side of the hearth wrapped in blankets.

"Theer's little use in saying pigs conner fly, when you see them catching swallows! But I dunner like the sound of it at all.

"And you say as you've to get our Bridestone to the top of Shuttlingslow by Friday morning? Well, that wunner be difficult. You two con stay here, if you've a mind to, and catch a bus from Macclesfield to Wildboarclough, and then all you'll have to do is climb up the hill and meet your wizard."

"We must take no such chances," said Fenodyree. "That would be a dangerous course; we shall go on foot."

"Well, I don't see it, myself," sniffed Bess.

"When do we start?" asked Susan.

"At dawn tomorrow. We dare not stay long in any place."

" 'We?' " said Bess. "Oh, no! If you think you're dragging these two childer off on your madcap errands you con think again!"

164

"Oh, but *Bess* . . . ! !"

"Aye, it's all very well saying 'but Bess'! What would your mother do if she knew of these goings on? She's enough to worry about as it is. And look at the state you were in this evening! You conner run risks like that and get away with it every time."

"Mistress Mossock," said Durathror, "the Stone-maiden and her brother *are* children, but they have warriors' hearts: they deserve well of this quest."

"That's as may be. But what should we say to their parents if they went out of here in the morning, and never came back? We're responsible for them, tha knows."

"If Colin and Susan do not see this through to the end in the company of those best fitted to help them," said Fenodyree, "their chances of ever setting eyes on parents or home again will be less than little. They have thwarted evil this day, and it will be a pledge of honor for witch and svart alike to make good that wrong. It would be madness to leave them unprotected here."

"Aye, I follow your meaning—if all we've heard is true," said Gowther. "Yon's a good point. But we're still responsible, choose how you look at it." He stood up to knock his pipe out against the bars of the grate. "I'll be coming with you in the morning."

As soon as the dwarfs were dressed, they wrapped themselves in their blankets and said they would sleep for a

165

couple of hours, but they were to be woken immediately at the least hint of trouble. They had already seen to it that everybody's bedding had been brought down into the kitchen, for they insisted that they should all stay in the one room that night, with ample supplies of food, light, and fuel.

At nine o'clock Durathror awoke and said he was going outside to see how the land lay.

He stole across the farmyard and up the hill to the top of the Riddings. The light northeaster that had been blowing for many days had veered to the north, and was much stronger. The full moon was rising in a clear sky; clear, except for the north. There banks of cloud were piling on the horizon, and Durathror frowned. He sniffed the air, and looked warily all about him.

"Wind's getting up a bit, inner it?" said Gowther when the dwarf returned.

"Aye: it is not a good wind: I have doubts."

Colin and Susan had dropped off to sleep very early, and by eleven o'clock Gowther and Bess were nodding in their chairs.

Shortly before midnight Scamp began to growl. It started as a distant rumble deep in his chest, and grew to a hard-throated snarl. His lips curled and his hackles rose. Durathror and Fenodyree quietly drew their swords and took up stations on either side of the door. Scamp barked, but Gowther hushed him and sent him under the table: yet still he whined, and growled, and rolled his eyes. All ears were straining to catch the least sound, but no sound came.

"Happen it's a fox," whispered Gowther.

Fenodyree shook his head.

"Something is coming: I can feel it."

"Mossock!" said a voice just outside the door. "Mossock, are you there?"

"It is the Place woman," whispered Durathror to Gowther.

"Aye, I'm here. What do you want?"

"You know what we want. Hand over to us the children, the dwarfs—and the stone, and you shall go unharmed."

"And supposing I tell thee to go and jump in the Bollin, what then?"

"Do not play the fool with us, Mossock. You have a minute in which to open this door before we break it, and you. Your house will fall, and weeds will grow on this land for a hundred years. Hurry! We are not usually so indulgent. Do not ask for trouble."

"Pay no heed: she is bluffing," said Fenodyree. "They cannot pass over a threshold unasked. It is an old binding spell stronger than any they can weave."

"Oh? Reet! Did you hear that, Mrs. Place? Well, to make it quite clear how we stond, here it is, straight and simple. *You conner come in!*"

There was a moment's silence before the Morrigan spoke again, and now her voice was soft, and more menacing than before.

"We did not expect it to be so easy. But do not deceive

167

yourselves by thinking that, because we cannot enter, you are safe. Wherever you are, and whatever you do, there is no escape; for we have called those to whom such spells are meaningless, and tomorrow night they will come to you. Listen, dwarfs! Can you not hear them? The mara are stirring. Soon they will be awake!"

16

THE WOOD OF RADNOR

ALONG THE CREST of the Riddings the morthbrood
watched Shape-shifter climb laboriously up from the farm.
Grimnir sat a little apart from the brood, while over the
top of the hill, in an old quarry, were mustered the svart-
alfar.

"They are all there," said the Morrigan. "And they will
not be drawn, though we think the threat of the mara will
bring them out once the night is gone. On the move, we
shall have them; but we must raise the fimbulwinter at
daybreak.

"Is Slinkveal here? Good. The svart-alfar will remain
in the quarry until dawn. You will not be needed, but
then again, you may.

"The watchers have been chosen, and know their duties.
Grimnir will accompany us to resume our work."

Durathror and Fenodyree kept watch by turns throughout the night, and at six o'clock they woke the others: by
seven all were ready to go. Day was near, and there was
a hard frost.

Colin, Susan, and Gowther were taking with them a change of clothing, food for the whole party, and ground-sheets. Fenodyree had made himself a cloak out of an old blanket.

They were about to shoulder their packs when there came a gentle knock at the door.

"Aye, who is it?" said Gowther.

"It's me, maister Mossock. Is owt up?"

"Oh, wait on a minute, Sam: I'll be reet with thee."

Gowther waited until the dwarfs had hidden in the next room before he drew the bolts and unlocked the door.

"Theer! Come in, lad. I was hoping you'd be here before I went."

"I saw the curtain were pulled to," said Sam Harlbutt, "and the sheds were fast, so I thowt as how happen summat was wrong."

"Oh no, theer's nowt wrong: but—er—I've been called away—er—sudden like, and young Colin and Susan are coming with me. We should be back by Saturday. Con you manage by yourself? I'll get John Carter to give thee a hond, if you like."

"Oh no, maister Mossock, I'll be all reet."

He showed not the least surprise.

"But I'd best get on with the milking pretty sharpish, hadn't I? Dick Thornicroft'll be here with his wagon in half an hour."

"Oh aye! Er—aye, you'd best do that now."

Gowther felt Sam's unspoken criticism, but could think

of no explanation to give him. It was their practice to share the milking, Gowther taking the morning, and Sam the evening. The cows ought to have been milked an hour ago, but Fenodyree would not let Gowther put his foot over the doorstep while it was still dark.

"Er—Sam, if Dick comes before you've finished, ask him to call when he's been to Barber's."

"Right-ho, maister Mossock."

"And Sam!"

"Aye?"

"When you've done milking, I'd like you to take Bess in the cart to her sister's at Big Tidnock: she'll be stopping theer while we come back. The dog'll be going, too."

"Oh, right-ho, maister Mossock."

Sam Harlbutt was as imperturbable as only a Cheshire man can be.

They waited until Sam was well into the milking before they slipped quietly out into the lane.

"Which way?" said Gowther.

"Let us first follow the road to the back of this hill," said Durathror. "From there we may see much to interest us."

The lane ran past the mouth of the quarry behind the Riddings, and Gowther was rather perplexed when Durathror suggested beginning their journey with a scramble about inside.

"It's nobbut an owd sond-hole. We shanner get far running round here!"

"We shall not be long," said the dwarf. "I want . . . ah!

171

As I thought! Svarts were here in the night, but I do not think there was much else with them. Come with me now to the hilltop."

He ran backwards and forwards along the Riddings like a hound beating for a scent.

"Nor was there aught worse than the morthbrood here. That is good. But yonder is what I do not like. Cousin Fenodyree, what make you of those clouds to the north? How is it they have not changed since I saw them under the moon? The wind should have carried them to us long ago."

"Hm," said the dwarf. "Fimbulwinter?"

"Aye. They do not mean to lose. First, they drive us out with the threat of the mara. We dare not bide. Next, they watch us through the day, and when we reach some lonely place, they pen us close under the fimbulwinter till night comes, and they can take us as they wish."

"Wait on," said Gowther; "what's all this 'fimbulwinter' business? And you've not told us yet . . ."

"I know," broke in Fenodyree. "But there are some things better left untold. It will be time enough to fear the mara when we see them: and I hope we shall not do that. Meanwhile you will rest happier for your ignorance."

"That makes me a *lot* easier, I must say!"

Fenodyree smiled, and inclined his head politely.

"You're a supercilious little feller when you want to be, anner you?" said Gowther testily. He was a direct, open man, who liked everything to be clearly defined. He could not tolerate haziness or uncertainty: and he had not quite overcome the countryman's natural distrust of strangers—such strangers, too!

"I do not mean to give offense," said the dwarf. "But I must ask you to lean on our judgment in this venture. You are in our world now, and without us you will not regain your own, even though it lies at your feet."

Gowther looked down at Highmost Redmanhey, then back at the dwarf. There was a long pause.

"Aye. I spoke out of turn. You're reet, and I'm wrong. I'm sorry."

"It is of no matter," said Fenodyree.

"Oh, look!" said Colin, anxious to change the subject. "We're not the only people out early this morning. There are two hikers down by Mr. Carter's: can you see them?"

In the lane below, a man and a woman, both knapsacked, and wearing anoraks, ski pants, and heavy boots, were leaning over a field gate, apparently absorbed in a map.

"There are two more behind us on Clinton hill," said Susan.

Sure enough, a quarter of a mile away, not much higher than where they were standing, two hikers gazed at the wide plain and its rim of hills.

"Happen it's a rally," said Gowther.

"Ha! It is indeed!" laughed Durathror shortly. "Those are witches and warlocks, or I am not my father's son!"

"What?" said Colin. "Are *they* the morthbrood?"

"There is the danger," said Fenodyree. "They mingle with others unnoticed, and can be detected only by certain marks, and that not always. For this reason must we shun all contact with men: the lonely places are dangerous, but to be surrounded by a crowd would be a greater risk."

Gowther shook his head, and pointed his ash stick at the "hikers."

"You mean to tell me it's the likes of them as we've to run from? I was thinking more of broomsticks and tall hats!"

The whale-backed Pennines, in their southern reaches, crumble into separate hills which join up with the Staffordshire moors, and from the Cheshire plain two hills stand out above all the rest. One is Bosley Cloud, its north face sheer, and southwards a graceful sweep to the feet of the Old Man of Mow, but, for all that, a brooding, sinister mountain, forever changing shape when seen from meandering Cheshire lanes.

The other is Shuttlingslow. It is a cone in outline, but with the top of the cone sliced off, leaving a flat, narrow, exposed ridge for a summit. And three days hence, on that ridge, eight miles from where they now were, Firefrost would be given into safe hands—if the morthbrood could be kept at bay for so long.

"Aye, and that's another thing," said Gowther. "What are we going to do between now and Friday? It's nobbut half a day's tramp to Shuttlingslow from here."

"Hush!" said Fenodyree. "There are keen ears listening. The where and the when are all they do not know of our plans. If we can shake off these bloodhounds and lie hidden

174

until nearer the time, we may reach the hill. Trees and running water will shield us best; and for a start we must try to lose the morthbrood spies in the wood that fringes Radnor mere. We shall keep to this lane until we come opposite the middle of the wood: there we shall enter and, with luck, come out at the far side alone."

"But we shall need more luck to remain alone," said Durathror, "for I fear that little escapes *those* eyes."

Above their heads wheeled a cloud of ragged-winged birds. Out over the plain other flocks were sweeping in what, from the height of the Riddings, could be seen to form a very definite pattern, an interwoven net of such efficiency that any one section of the ground of, say, a mile square, was rarely left uncovered by any one flock for more than a minute at a time. And they flew in silence, the only living things in all the sky. The hikers continued to pore over the map, and to admire the view.

Fenodyree led the way back to the crossroads, where the old Macclesfield road, Hocker Lane, ran left to Highmost Redmanhey, and right to Nether Alderley. To Alderley they turned, and walked beneath the round shoulder of Clinton hill. Below, across the fields, was Radnor Wood.

"I'll tell you what," said Gowther. "Tom Henshaw seems to be as mithered with these birds as much as we are: he's getten enough scarecrows, anyroad."

"Aye," said Durathror, "and can you tell me, farmer Mossock, what need he may have of them on pastureland?"

It was as Durathror said. Every field within sight held a tattered figure with outstretched arms—even those under grass, and with cows in them.

"Now I wonder what's up with owd Tom! He did say as how he'd been having queer turns off and on since before Christmas, but this is . . ."

"No time to linger," said Fenodyree. "You will embarrass our companions."

They looked around, and saw that the two hikers who had been leaning over John Carter's gate were now walking casually along some distance behind, to all appearances engaged in nothing more sinister than knocking off the tops of dead fool's-parsley with their sticks. A flock of thirteen birds closed in and began to glide in circles overhead.

"*Are* they scarecrows?" asked Colin as they continued down the lane.

"Mostly," said Fenodyree: "but eyes for the morthbrood, every one."

The road gradually converged on Radnor wood until the two were running together, with only a low stone wall between them, and at a bend in the road Fenodyree said:

"When the morthdoers round this corner, we must be hidden.

"Now! Over the wall!"

Brambles were waiting for them on the other side, but they tore themselves free, and ran as best they could through the scrub and undergrowth of the matted fringe of the wood after Fenodyree, who was dodging nimbly over the

176

rough ground and heading for the thickest patch of timber in sight.

At once the birds began to raise a great rumpus, but Durathror, bringing up the rear as usual, saw nothing of the hikers before the trees closed around him.

As soon as they were in the shade of the beeches the prickly undergrowth thinned out, and they made good speed, zigzagging through the lessening gaps between the trees and the masses of rhododendron. For a short time the birds screamed overhead and then they dropped through the branches and circled in and out among the trees, calling assuredly, deliberately, as though relaying information.

Fenodyree relaxed the pace to a quick walk.

"There is no need to hurry," he said resignedly. "I hoped to find cover while they pondered. This wood did not favor the morthbrood in the elder days, and I thought the memory of it would hold them long enough for . . ."

His words were drowned by an outbreak of screeching above their heads. Instinctively they drew together, back to back, and the dwarfs' hands flew to their swords. All around them birds were crashing heavily to earth: for ten seconds it might have been raining crows. Then the woods were still.

Gowther bent to pick up a tumbled mass of black feathers that had landed at his feet, but Durathror stopped him.

"Do not touch it!" he said. "They are evil even in death."

He turned the bird over with the point of his sword.

177

Imbedded under the heart was a small, white-feathered arrow; and at the sight of it all color fled from Durathror's cheeks.

"The lios-alfar," he whispered. "The lios-alfar!"

Trembling, he put away his sword, and looked to the sky.

"Endil! Atlendor! It is I, Durathror! This is well met!"

"Peace!" said Fenodyree. "They are not here."

"Are they not?" cried Durathror. "Ho! I tell you, cousin Wineskin, that our journey will be happier from this hour. If the lios-alfar are come from exile there is little *we* need fear between now and Friday's dawn, do you not *see?*

"Atlendor, welcome! Airmid! Grannos!"

But for all Durathror's shouting, nothing happened. He ran hither and thither calling, calling, but echoes and the hollow voice of the north wind in the treetops were his only reply.

"Thrurin! Skandar!"

Fenodyree shook his head sadly.

"Come away. The lios-alfar have been gone from the Long Wood of Radnor these two hundred years. They do not return. Come! They are not here: none but the morthbrood will answer your call."

Durathror walked slowly back to join the others.

"But it can be only the lios-alfar." There was complete bewilderment in his voice. "Why do they not know me?"

178

Fenodyree crouched to examine the arrow more closely.

"Well, whoever fired yon, conner be much of a size," said Gowther. "If it's eighteen inches long that's all it is, and what sort of a body could use the bow to fit it?"

"The elves of light," said Fenodyree, "The lios-alfar. This is an elven shaft. Yet still I do not think they are with us. It is more like to be the work of stromkarls."

"*Stromkarls?*" cried Durathror. "Have you ever known the river-folk to take up arms? It is the lios-alfar!"

"Eh up! What's yon?" said Gowther, and pointed into the trees.

Something white moved among the branches, though not even Gowther could say where it first appeared. It fell gently toward them, swinging backwards and forwards with a graceful, swooping, dipping motion, and landed at Durathror s feet. A white eagle feather.

The dwarf grabbed it, and flourished it under his cousin's nose.

"*See!* A token! And from an elven cloak! What say you now?"

Fenodyree looked hard at the feather, and then at Durathror.

"It is the lios-alfar," he said.

Fenodyree urged them on with all speed after the delay. No other sign from the elves, if they *were* elves, was forthcoming, and Durathror was prevailed upon to curb his excitement, and to turn his thoughts to their immediate problems.

179

"But it is hard," he said to Colin later in the day, when they were sharing the same cloak in an effort to stay alive, "it is hard to lose the companionship of elves. And if one has been dearer to you than your own kin, a more than brother right from earliest memory, the loss is nigh unbearable. When Atlendor took his people northwards I thought to renounce my heritage, and go with him, but he would not have me come. 'You have a duty to discharge,' he said, 'one of great weight.' The eyes of the lios-alfar see not only the present. By Goldenstone we said our farewells, and he gave to me Valham, and I parted with Tarnhelm, the greatest treasure of the huldrafolk." Durathror smiled ruefully. "I exchanged the power of going unseen for the power of flight, and Gondemar, my father, cast me out in his anger. So have I wandered all these years, barred from my people and from the elves. Had not Cadellin pitied me, and opened to me the gates of Fundindelve, mine would have been a desolate lot."

But all this came much later in the day, and for the present the children and Gowther were left to make what sense they could of the dead birds and Durathror's ravings.

Not that there was time for thought. They were forcing their way down an almost extinct track of frozen, rutted leaf-mold, between rhododendrons of such size that the branches met over their heads as well as across their path, when Fenodyree held up his hand. They stopped; listened.

"Footsteps! Into the bushes!"

They forced their way through the glossy hide of leaves into the tangled, bare branches that comprised the main bulk of the growth.

"Stay wherever you are, and do not move!" whispered Durathror fiercely. "He is close."

It was difficult to see through the bushes in the dappled light. They heard someone approach, but caught only a glimpse of dark clothing. Whoever it was, he was breathing heavily. Then, as he came level with where they were hiding, he stopped. Colin, Susan, and Gowther prayed that the beating of their hearts was not as loud as it sounded Durathor and Fenodyree exchanged glances.

"Phew! Be hanged to old Place!" muttered a deep voice, and the owner of it sat himself down on the trunk of a fallen beech that lay across the path: and in that position his face could be seen. It was Mr. Hodgkins, a local businessman.

Every morning during the week, between the hours of eight and nine, he was to be found, with dozens like him, on the platform of Alderley Edge station, carrying his briefcase and tightly folded newspaper, and tightly rolled umbrella. But now, in place of the stiff white collar and formal, city clothes, James Henry Hodgkins's frame was clad in thick ski pants, and a hooded anorak, above which protruded the neck of a sweater. A beret hid his thinning hair, around his lean neck were snow goggles, leather gauntlets hung by tapes from his wrist, nailed boots encumbered his feet, and down his lined, sallow, businessman's face ran

181

rivulets. He put his back against the roots of the tree, took out his handkerchief, and began to mop.

Five pairs of eyes watched him in agony. Neither the children, Gowther, nor the dwarfs had had time to make themselves comfortable among the branches, even if that were possible, but were standing frozen in the most awkward attitudes, cramped, precariously balanced. Any movement would have set the leaves dancing at the end of their snake-like branches. It was as though they were dangling in a snarl of burglar alarms. However, James Henry was not one to waste time unduly, and as soon as he was restored to a more even temperature he pulled himself up and went on his way, cursing the unwieldly knapsack that chafed his shoulders and was always becoming entangled with the bushes.

"Well!" said Gowther. "Owd Hodgkins! Ten years he's been a customer of mine. It just shows, you con never tell."

"I didn't breathe once the whole time!" said Susan.

"I *couldn't!*" said Colin. "There was a branch twisting my collar, and it nearly strangled me! It's not much better now. Is it safe to move yet, Fenodyree?"

"Aye, if we can," said the dwarf.

He was wrestling to free his leg, which was hooked around the knee by a branch. But the branch swung higher at every jerk, and Fenodyree was being tipped gradually backwards off his feet. He looked so ridiculous, his knee level with his ear, that the others would have been

182

tempted to laugh at his plight, had not they found themselves in difficulties as soon as they tried to move.

These were old bushes, and behind the green outer cover lay the growth and litter of a hundred years; tough, crooked boughs, inches across, stemming to long, pliant, wire-like shoots; skeins of dead branches which snapped at a touch, forming lancets of wood to goad and score the flesh; and everywhere the fine, black, bark dust with the bitter taste, that burned throat and nostrils and was like fine sand in the eyes.

"It's as . . . bad . . . as walking . . . on an old . . . spring mattress!" puffed Susan.

"It's worse!" said Colin.

They had to step onto the thicker branches to clear the snare at ground level, and once off the ground they were helpless. The bushes dictated the direction in which they could move, and movement was not easy. Branches would give beneath their feet, and spring back awkwardly, catching limbs, and making even Gowther, for all his weight, lurch drunkenly, and grab in desperation the nearest support, which was invariably a change for the worse. And always they seemed to be forced to climb, with the result that they were soon two or three feet from the ground. Sense of direction left them: they just took the line of least resistance. But they noticed, with growing concern, that the earth, or what they could see of it, was becoming less like earth and more like water. Ice-covered puddles were fre-

183

quent; very frequent; broader; deeper; they joined each other; and then there was water tinkling the pendants of ice at the bush roots, and no earth at all. Ahead, the curtain was not so dense, and Fenodyree, with renewed enthusiasm, plunged, bounced, rolled, and squirmed, and his head broke free of the chaos. Before, on either side, beneath, lay Radnor. The rhododendrons spread for many yards out over the mere, their roots gripping deep in the mud; and at the point where they stretched farthest into the water, five faces bobbed among the leaves like exotic flowering buds.

"Happen I'm nesh," said Gowther, "but I dunner foncy a dip today. I'm fair sick of this here cakewalk, though; so what do we do, maister?"

"Nay, do not ask me, my friend. I am past thought," said Durathror.

"We must go back," said Fenodyree. "Cousin, we may have space to draw our swords here. If we can do that, we shall cut an easier road to the path."

Dyrnwyn and Widowmaker, after much effort, were drawn from their scabbards, and by leaning backwards over the water, the dwarfs gained room for the first, most difficult strokes. After that, in comparison with what had gone before, the progress was much easier. The dead growth, and the leaf-bearing tentacles fell to the keen temper of the swords, which left only the thicker limbs to be negotiated, and they were not the obstacles they had been when the all-smothering lesser branches were there to aid

184

them. The real danger, and it was a risk that had to be taken, was that the dwarfs were carving a track that could not fail to be visible from the air.

"Now we must run," said Fenodyree as, hot, weary, smarting from a hundred pricks and scratches, they tumbled onto the path. "For the morthbrood know where we are."

Only when they had put much dense woodland behind them did Fenodyree allow a few minutes for rest.

"Are we making for anywhere in particular?" asked Colin.

"Not for the moment," said Fenodyree. "I have a place in mind that may be the saving of us—if we can reach it. But I shall not speak of that while there is danger of hidden ears."

"Cousin," said Durathror, "do you hear?"

They fell silent, tensely listening.

"Aye; it is an ax."

They could all hear it now—the clear, rhythmical ring of steel in timber.

Gowther relaxed.

"I know who yon is," he said. "It'll be Harry Wardle from the Parkhouse. He's all reet. I've known him since we were lads. If theer's been onybody in this end of the wood today, it's as like as not he'll have seen 'em. Let's ask him."

"Hm," said Durathror. "I would rather not meet with men at this time: trust no one."

185

"But Harry and I were at school together: he's a good lad."

"He may be all you think," said Fenodyree. "If he is, he may be able to help us. Speak with him: Durathror and I shall watch. If he is of the morthbrood he will not raise the alarm."

They halted at the edge of a clearing. A lean, bony, middle-aged man, with close-cropped, iron-gray hair, was standing with his back to them, and wielding a long-handled felling ax.

"How do, Harry," said Gowther.

Harry Wardle turned, and smiled.

"Hello, Gowther! What's brought thee down here?"

"Oh, I'm just out for the day with young Colin and Susan here."

"Eh, you farmers! I wish I could take time off when I wanted! How is the farm these days?"

"Middling, for the time of the year, tha knows. Could be worse."

"And Bess?"

"She's champion, thanks. Busy morning, Harry?"

"Fair. Couple more trees to drop after this before dinner: but I'll be having baggin after this one's down. Care for some?"

He nodded toward the flask and sandwiches that were lying on a tree stump.

"No; thanks, Harry, all the same, but we mun be getting on."

186

"Just as you please. Going far?"

"I dunner know: as far as we've a mind to, I expect. Mony folks about today, Harry?"

"Not a soul, till you come along."

"Well, if onbody does show up, you hanner seen us, reet?"

A slow grin spread over Harry Wardle's face.

"I've never clapped eyes on thee, Gowther. What's up? Are you fancying a cock pheasant or two? Because if you are, take a look round Painter's Eye; but dunner say to onybody as I told thee."

Gowther winked slyly.

"Be good, Harry."

"Be good, lad."

They waved, and left him, and a moment later the sound of his ax rang out behind them through the trees.

"Well?" said Gowther. "What did I say?"

"He is no warlock," said Fenodyree, "but there is that about him I do not trust: it would have been wiser to pass him by."

"Hush!" said Durathror. "Listen!"

"I can't hear anything," said Colin.

"Nor me," said Gowther.

"But you *should* hear something!" cried Fenodyree. *"Why has your friend's ax been stilled?"*

"Eh? What?" said Gowther, suddenly flustered. "Here! Howd on a minute!"

But Durathror and Fenodyree were speeding back toward the clearing, drawing their swords as they ran.

The clearing was empty. Harry Wardle, ax, flask, and food, were gone.

"But . . ." stammered Gowther, his face purple, "but . . . it's not . . . no, not *Harry*. No! He'll have nipped back to the Parkhouse for summat, that's what!"

"If that were so," said Fenodyree, "he would have come up with us, for we were heading for the Parkhouse, were we not?"

"Aye, I suppose we were." Gowther looked stunned.

Durathror, who had taken the path on the other side of the clearing, returned, shaking his head.

"As you say, farmer Mossock," said Fenodyree, "you can never tell."

17

MARA

"We must not act rashly," said Fenodyree. "Fear is our enemies' greatest ally."

"Aye," said Gowther, "but let's be moving, shall we? I dunner mind admitting I've had a shock; and stonding here talking while who knows what may be creeping up on us inner improving things."

"But which way shall we go now in least danger?" said Fenodyree. "That is what we must decide. I put no trust in blind flight, and though time is precious, a little may be well spent in counsel. Remember, your Harry may have to travel some distance to give his warning."

"Well, they know what direction we're following now, don't they?" said Colin. "And I don't suppose Harry Wardle realizes we're onto him, so why not double back on our tracks?"

"That is good," said Durathror. "The hares will dart north while the hounds run south."

"I think . . . not," said Fenodyree. "It is a good plan in many ways, but we have too great a charge to take the risk. Consider: it is probable that the body of the morth-brood is to our rear. They will come southwards through this wood, and along its flanks. If we lie in the thicket, and they pass by, ours will be the advantage. But if we should be found, far from help, unable to wield a sword for the dense growth, what need then of fimbulwinter or the mara? And if we should win through their line un-noticed, our way would grow more perilous. North of here lie villages: too many men. South, the land is open for ten miles and more. We are not far from the southern boundary of this wood: let us hurry southwards. If we are clear of Radnor before the alarm has spread, the morth-brood may waste time in sitting round to mark where we run clear."

So it was agreed; they walked swiftly, and carefully, close together, and the swords were naked.

Durathror kept glancing upwards at the patches of blue sky. He was troubled. Then he began to sniff the air.

"Is it near, cousin?" asked Fenodyree.

"It is. An hour, two hours: not more."

"Yon warlock, with his snow-garments, removed any doubts," said Fenodyree to Gowther and the children. "The morthbrood have called Rimthur to their aid, and the ice-giant's breath, the fimbulwinter, is upon us. We must bear it if we can."

The curtness of his speech told them more than the words. He was pale beneath his nut-brown skin, and even Gowther felt in no need of further explanation.

190

After they had skirted the Parkhouse and its outbuildings the wood declined into timbered parkland, which thinned to open fields, and under the last cluster of trees, the dwarfs halted to consider the next move. To their right was the Congleton road, bordered by a stone wall. On their side of the wall a belt of woodland followed the road, and the open ground between where they were crouching and this thicker cover was sparsely dotted with trees. A flock of birds wheeled overhead. No human figures were to be seen; the intermittent buzz of traffic on the road was the only noise beyond the wind.

"Where may our way lead now?" said Durathror.

"It's a deal too exposed for me," said Gowther. "And if we carry on we come to Monks' Heath, which is a sight worse. But howd on a minute: let's have a look round. It's a while since I was round here. I wish them birds would give it a rest!" He scanned the country before them. "It'd be better if we could reach them trees by the wall; aye, yon's the best road. Sithee; they go reet down the wall, and bend across to Dumville's plantation, and that'll take us round the edge of Monks' Heath to Bag brook. From theer we may—we *may*—be able to nip across to the game coverts by Marlheath at Capesthorne. It's these next two hundred yards as is going to be the biggest snag. But happen if we keep an eye open for birds we con pick our time and dodge about a bit till we're theer."

And that is what they did. Choosing a moment when

191

the sky was clear, they darted toward the road like frantic ants, weaving from tree to tree in bursts of speed that amazed Gowther: he had not run like this for thirty years. But they reached the strip of woodland before the next patrol flew by.

The trees left the road almost at right angles and continued across the fields as what Gowther called Dumville's plantation. For most of its length it was very narrow, only a matter of feet in places, but it gave splendid cover from the air. After half a mile the wood swung right and headed south once more: it curved over the brow of a low hill, and from there a good view of the surrounding country was obtained.

"It's well wooded, at any rate," said Susan.

"But it will appear bare to you for most of our journey," laughed Fenodyree. "Things are not as they were: in the elder days ours would have been an easier task. There were true forests then."

"I wonder who yon is on Sodger's Hump," said Gowther.

They all looked. A mile away, above the crossroads on Monk's Heath, a grassy hill stood out above the land. It was like a smaller Shuttlingslow—or a tumulus. It had the tumulus's air of mystery; it was subtly different from the surrounding country; it *knew* more than the fields in which it had its roots. And this uneasy mood was heightened by a group of Scots pines that crowned the summit. They leaned toward each other, as though sharing secrets. And outlined among the trees was a man on horseback.

192

Little detail could be seen at that distance, but the children thought that he was probably wearing a cloak, and possibly a hat. He sat completely motionless.

"I . . . cannot tell who he is," said Durathror, after much peering. "There is that about him that strikes a chord of memory. What think you, cousin?"

Fenodyree shook his head.

"It could, and could not, be one I know. It would be strange to find *him* here. It is almost certain to be a warlock guarding the crossroad."

But, for some time after, the dwarfs were withdrawn, and pensive.

The trees dropped to the Macclesfield road in the hollow where it crossed Bag brook, and, dividing his attention between birds and traffic, Fenodyree was kept busy for a good ten minutes while he shepherded the others to the opposite side of the road and under the bridge arch. This accomplished, the dwarfs, for the first time since the disappearance of Harry Wardle, put away their swords.

"I begin to have hope of this quest," said Fenodyree. "We are well clear of Radnor, and I think the morthbrood have lost the trail."

"Aye, but I hope we dunner have to stay under this bridge all day, patting ourselves on the back," said Gowther. "I wouldner say as this mud is over fresh, would you?"

"We shall move at once!" said Fenodyree.

"Here is what we shall attempt. North of Shuttlingslow lies Macclesfield forest, as wild a region as any on the

193

hills; but men have covered much of it with spruce and fir. Do you know it?"

"Aye," said Gowther. "It starts above Langley reservoirs. I dunner reckon much to it, though—mile after mile of trees on parade; it inner natural."

"That is the place; a dungeon of trees. But their sad ranks grow thickly, and there is little chance of finding aught that hides within. The forest will keep us till Friday's dawn, when we shall climb over the last mile of moorland to Shuttlingslow."

"As easy as that?" said Gowther.

"*If* we can gain the forest," said Durathror.

Fenodyree's plan was to head south for a few miles before turning east, and to travel, wherever possible, through woods. The intervening stretches of country, he hoped, would be crossed by following the lines of streams. Ignoring discomfort, the advantages of this plan were many. Along the streams, alder and willow were certain to be found, linked by lesser growth, reeds, rushes, and straggling elder. Moving lower than the adjacent fields would make for greater stealth, since there would be no danger of being outlined against the sky. And, in the last resort, it would be possible to lie close under the bank if caught in the open by the approach of birds. Also running water kills scent, which might be important, for there were still two of the hounds of the Morrigan left alive.

All this Fenodyree explained; his plan was accepted without dissent, and they now began the most arduous part of their journey, falling into a pattern of movement that was

194

to govern them for slow, exhausting miles. They had to keep together as a body, yet move and act as individuals, each responsible for finding, and gaining, cover before birds were overhead, and pushing on as soon as the sky was clear. Desperate scrambles, long periods of inactivity, mud, sand, water, ice, malicious brambles; one mile an hour was good progress.

The brook led them southwest, toward the left of Sodger's Hump, and inevitably crossing under the Congleton road, which was not at all to anybody's liking. However, a few yards short of the bridge, though still dangerously close, a tributary joined Bag brook. It flowed in an acute angle from the left, from the direction of the Capestorne game covert. This meant that they were almost doubling back on their tracks, but it promised to be such an accommodating route that no one regretted the lost ground or wasted energies: it was worth all that to be traveling in exactly the right line—an experience that was to prove all too rare. Not long after turning up this smaller brook they saw the first hikers on the fringe of Dumville's plantation.

The brook came from a valley of birch scrub and dead bracken; this was an improvement on bare fields, but ahead towered a sanctuary of larches, and the crawl seemed endless.

"By the ribbons of Frimla!" said Durathror when they were beneath the laced branches. "It is good to drop that coward's gait and walk on two legs."

"I only hope the birds are deaf," said Susan.

195

The ground was covered inches deep with dead larch twigs and small branches. It was impossible not to tread on them, and, with five pairs of feet on the move, dwarfs and humans passed through that wood with a sound like a distant forest fire.

From the larches they crossed a small area of scrub to a plantation of firs—specimens of Gowther's despised "trees on parade." But these trees were well grown, and there were few low branches. The floor was mute: no sun cut through the green roof: here twilight lay hidden at noon. Everybody was more at ease than at any time since leaving Highmost Redmanhey.

"It's a treat not to think eyes are boring into your shoulder blades, inner it?" said Gowther.

"And to be out of the sun," said Colin. "It was trained on us like a spotlight."

"Well, the light's certainly dim enough in here," said Susan. "It's taken till now for my eyes to get used to the change."

"I mun be still a bit mazed, then," said Gowther, "for to my way of thinking it's coming on darker instead of lighter."

"It is," said Fenodyree.

The wood broke on the foot of a small hillock, and there all was plain to see.

The blue sky and brilliant sun had vanished. From horizon to horizon the air was black and yellow with unbroken clouds.

"These are but the outriders," said Durathror. "Do we stay here beneath shelter, or move on?"

"On," said Fenodyree. "While we may."

A path took them through the covert, past many green pools; and, at a plank that spanned a boundary ditch, all shelter ended. Before them was parkland, the nearest wood a quarter of a mile away across open country that offered no scrap of cover.

"Well, that's that, inner it?" said Gowther. "What do we do now? Wait while night?"

Fenodyree shook his head.

"We must not travel in the dark; not when we are so far from help. We shall move soon. The storm is at hand, and at its height it will pluck even the morthbrood from the sky. Then shall we cross."

They did not have to wait. The first snow whipped by as Fenodyree finished speaking, and the next moment the world had shrunk to a five-yard circle, shot through with powdered ice, and bounded by a wall and ceiling of leaping gray.

"Naught can find us in this!" shouted Fenodyree against the skirl of the wind. "Now is our chance!"

Once they were out of the shelter of the wood the full weight of the storm flung itself upon them. Susan, Colin, and the dwarfs were picked up and thrown to the ground, while Gowther lurched as though he had been stunned. They groped their way together, and linked arms, Gowther in the middle as anchor, and the wind frog-marched them at a giant-striding run direct to their goal.

It was the shallowest of valleys. They bounced over the edge, and were dropped by the storm as it leaped across the gap. Close to where they landed a fallen tree threw up soil-clogged roots, a natural shield against the wind.

"We shall fare no better than this," said Fenodyree, "and we cannot battle with such a storm, so let us make the most of what we have."

At first it was enough to be out of the storm's reach: the snow hissed past, and little settled. But the air was cruel; and behind the roots there was not much space for five people to move, so they crouched and stood by turns, and the breath froze on their lips, and their eyelashes were brittle with ice.

The children pulled on all their spare clothing, and huddled to share the dwarfs' cloaks. Gowther came off worst. He had to make do with sticking his feet into the knapsack, and wrapping himself about with the clammy, cold, rubber-scented groundsheets. It was then that Durathror spoke of the lios-alfar, and of his friendship with Atlendor.

"But why should the elves leave here in the first place, and where did they go?" asked Colin when the tale was ended.

"The lios-alfar," said Durathror, "are the elves of light, creatures of air, the dew drinkers. To them beauty is food and life, and dirt and ugliness, death. When men turned from the sun and the earth, and corrupted the air with the smoke of furnaces, it was poison to the lios-alfar; the scab of brick and tile that spread over this land withered their hearts. They had to go, or die. Wherever men now were, there were noise and grime; only in the empty places was

198

there peace. Some of the lios-alfar fled to the mountains of Sinadon, some to the Isle of Iwerdon across the West-water, and others past the Depths of Dinsel in the south. But most went north with Atlendor to far Prydein, even beyond Minith Bannawg, and there they dwell upon the high hills. Now some, at least, have come south, but to what end I cannot tell, nor why they are hidden from me. But there can be no evil in it, that much is certain."

During the afternoon the wind dropped, and the roots were now no shelter from the snow. It fell steadily, monotonously, so that it seemed to the half-frozen figures behind the tree as though they were on a platform that moved upwards through a white, beaded curtain. Reality, space, and time dissolved in the blank, soaring, motionless world. Only an occasional squall drew back the curtain for a second or two, and destroyed the hypnotic illusion.

Toward nightfall Fenodyree made up his mind. Ever since the wind had ceased to clamp them behind the tree roots he had been weighing the advantages, and disadvantages, of moving on. As things stood, they were more than likely to lose their way, and they were dangerously close to Alderley, and to the Edge. No, that was a risk he did *not* want to take. But, on the other hand, it was becoming obvious that they could not all survive the night in the open. Already they were experiencing the fatal, warm drowsiness of exposure, and the mesmerism of the snow was undermining their resistance to the peril. Both Gowther and Colin had had to be roused more than once.

"We must move," said Fenodyree. "If we do not find a

199

roof for our heads we shall not have need of one by morning. I shall see if there is better cover downstream. The fewer tracks we make in this snow the safer we shall rest, but it would not be wise to go alone. Farmer Mossock, will you come with me?"

"I will that!" said Gowther. "I've about had enough of this place!"

Fenodyree and Gowther disappeared through the curtain.

They followed the valley for a quarter of a mile, and came to a cart track near to where it joined the Congleton road on their right.

"Hey!" said Gowther. "I know wheer we are! Straight on'll be Redesmere, and theer's some pretty thick woods just ahead: it's mainly rhododendron again, but happen we con make ourselves summat out of it. It's the best we'll find round these parts."

"It may be better than you think, my friend!" said the dwarf, his eyes gleaming. "I had given no thought to Redesmere."

They retraced their steps. All the time, Gowther had been at pains to put his feet exactly in Fenodyree's tracks, and his boots had blotted out the dwarf's smaller prints. Going back, they trod the same tracks as on the outward journey, and the result would give any hunter much to think about.

The snow was now a foot deep all over, and considerably more where it had drifted.

"We shall cut branches here and there to make a thatch,

if nothing better comes of Redesmere," said Fenodyree. "But we must not waste a moment, since it is past sunset already, and that is danger even before the coming of night. If we are to . . . ah! !"

"What . . . ?"

"Sh! *Look!*"

In the time that had elapsed since they passed that spot on the way to Redesmere *something* had crossed their path, leaving tracks like nothing Gowther had ever seen in all his days. A shallow furrow, two yards wide, had been swept through the snow, and along the center of the furrow ran the print of bare feet. Each foot was composed of a pointed big toe, divided by a cleft from the single wedge that filled the place where the other four toes would normally have been. The prints were evenly spaced—three yards apart.

"Hurry!" gasped Fenodyree. "And may we come in time!"

He did not draw his sword.

"I've a real snow-thirst," said Susan. "More than anything else at this moment I'd like a gallon of milk."

"Oh, don't," groaned Colin. "A gallon would only wet my lips!"

The stream water was too cold to drink: it numbed their throats, and made their teeth ache. And their mouths were dry and sweet with fatigue.

They spoke little, for conversation had died long ago:

201

it took too much effort. They moved only when cramp demanded.

After Gowther and Fenodyree had been gone about twenty minutes, Susan, developing pins and needles in all her limbs, got up to stamp around and flap her arms. She was on the point of crouching down again when she heard a faint swishing sound, as of somebody wading through the snow. Thinking the others were returning, she stood on tiptoe to peer out of the valley. This brought her eyes just above ground level; and at that moment a flurry of wind pulled aside the veil of snow. A second later the wind had gone by, and the veil fell back into place, but in that instant, Susan's eyes had registered every detail of the thing that was passing within ten yards of where she stood.

It bore some resemblance to a woman, an ill-proportioned woman, twenty feet high, and green. The long, thick-set trunk rested on massive legs with curving, bloated thighs. The arms were too short, muscular at the shoulders, but tapering to puny, indeterminate hands. The head was very small, elliptical, and scarcely broader than the neck on which it sat. There was no hair; the mouth was a shadowed line; the nose cut sharply down from the brow, between eyes that were no more than dark smears. It wore a single garment, a loose tunic that reached to the ground, and clung to the body in folds like wet linen. The flesh gleamed dully, and the tunic, of the same color and texture, might have been of the same substance. A statue of polished malachite; but a statue that moved.

Susan began to scream, but before the sound reached her lips, a rough hand was clapped over her mouth, and Durathror pushed her down into the snow.

"Lie still!"

For a time, above the beating of her heart, she felt the earth shake beneath a ponderous tread that died away.

"Did you see it?" she whispered.

"I saw it. We must find my cousin: next time our luck may not hold."

"What is it? What's wrong?" said Colin from the bottom of the slope. But as he spoke Fenodyree, with Gowther on his heels, staggered out of the gloom and caught Durathror by the arm.

"Mara!"

"It has this instant gone by," said Durathror. "It did not see us: there is still too much light."

"So did it miss our tracks. Come: we have found shelter."

"Then why do we delay?"

They slipped down the valley as quickly as they dared.

"Is curiosity satisfied now, farmer Mossock?" said Fenodyree when Susan had given a breathless description of what she had seen.

"Aye, it is that! But what in creation *are* they?"

"Troll-women: from rock are they spawned, and to rock they return if the sun should find them above ground. But by night they are indestructible, all-powerful. Only our wits can save us now, and be thankful we have more

203

than they, for the mara's brain is as meager as its strength is great."

The words were barely out of his mouth when a thin cry, like the plaintive voice of a night bird, yet cold and pitiless as the fangs of mountains, came from behind them.

"Run! It has found our trail!"

They had crossed the path where Fenodyree had turned back, and were forcing a way between the bushes when the mara called a second time, and now it was near.

"Steady!" cried Gowther. "We munner get separated in here!"

The thicket was not impenetrable, but it was close enough to make it difficult for five people to move quickly through it together. The snow was no longer falling: it was almost night.

Again the voice.

"Stay!" cried Durathror.

They had all heard: it was not an echo. It was an answering call—from in front!

Immediately there came another from the right, and the sound of snapping branches and rustling undergrowth. Hemmed in on three sides, they were, for the moment, spared the anguish of decision. They swung left. The voices were continuous now.

Durathror ran ahead of the rest. Susan was nearest to him, trying to keep in his wake, and as they came to a thick screen of brush, Durathror put up his arms to shield his eyes, and forced his way through. Susan's dive after him was halted by a stifled cry from Durathror, followed by a splash.

"What's happened?"

"Where are we?"

"What is it?"

"Are you all right?"

Susan put her head through the gap—and looked out across an apparently limitless sheet of water. In the gathering darkness she could not see any land. Beneath her, to his waist in the water, Durathror struggled to climb back through the weeds and dead vegetation to the land. By this time the others had all reached the spot.

"*Redesmere!*" said Gowther savagely. "I should have thowt of that one!"

"Back!" spluttered Durathror.

"But we conner!"

"We have no choice," said Fenodyree, "and very little time. We may pass through the net: we may."

Without a word Colin turned, and the rest hurried after.

"Colin, wait! Let me lead you!" Fenodyree called softly.

"All right . . . oh!"

"*Colin! !*"

"Stop, everybody!" cried Colin. "There's water here, too!"

"*What?* Theer conner be! Here, wait on a minute!"

Gowther turned off left, and plunged into the bushes: ten seconds later he was back, only to vanish in the opposite direction without speaking. When he reappeared he was walking very slowly.

"I dunner ask onybody to believe this," he said, "but we're on an island."

18

ANGHARAD GOLDENHAND

"AND IT INNER very big, either," said Gowther.

"But . . . but . . . it *can't* be an island!" said Susan.

"I know it conner: but it is."

"It's not *possible!*" said Colin.

"That's reet."

"But . . ."

Laughter broke in on their bewilderment, and they were aware of the dwarfs sitting in the snow, each with his back against a tree, at ease, and openly amused.

"It is in truth an island," said Durathror. "And, by the blade of Osla! I did not look to such a fair ending to this day's work."

"Hush!" said Fenodyree. "And lie low awhile."

On the nearer shore, fifty yards away, three mara were casting about to pick up the vanished scent. They wailed, and whooped, and peered at the ground, uprooting bushes and bending trees.

Gowther pressed himself farther into the snow: he was exposed, and obvious: it could not be long before the mara would put two and two together, and wade out to the island, and then . . .

Having flattened everything for yards around, the three shapes stood on the lake side, facing out across the water.

This is it, thought Susan. How far can I swim in these clothes? But the mara did not move: their bodies merged into the shadows. All was quiet. And then they turned, and disappeared into the wood: the whooping broke out again, and continued until all sounds were lost in the distance.

Gowther stood up, and shook the snow out of his clothes.

"They must be pretty dim!" said Colin. "Why didn't they find us? Anyone with half an eye could have guessed where we were: our footprints must have ended at the water."

"But the mara have not half a *mind*," said Fenodyree. "Our tracks were all they had to follow, and when they ended the trail was lost. Nothing was moving on the lake, there were no tracks, therefore there was nothing to find: so their minds work. They will wander now until dawn, and let us hope there are few men abroad this night."

"Yes, but they knew we were somewhere close," said Susan. "Why didn't they try this island?"

"Ah, but they did not *know*: they have never seen us. All they have seen are tracks that end in water. For the mara that is no puzzle; their minds look no farther than their eyes, and I think that to their eyes this island is hidden."

"Is it now?" said Gowther heavily. "You dunner sur-

208

prise me in the least! Happen you con also tell us how we come to be here without wetting our feet, *and* how we're going to get back to land again!"

"I do not doubt that we shall walk from here at sunrise," said Fenodyree, "and, meanwhile, sleep safely and well."

"This is the Isle of Angharad Goldenhand, the Lady of the Lake, and it is one of the Two Floating Islands of Logris. It was lodged against the shore when Angharad guided our feet thither. Here no evil will threaten us. For one night we may lie at peace, and the Lady will watch over us."

"Very comforting!" said Gowther. Melting snow was sliding down the inside of his collar, and he was tired. "But wheer is this 'lady' of thine? I conner see owt but snow and trees, and I doubt *they* wunner make a warm bed!"

"She is here, though we do not see her, and we are under her protection. Now we must eat a little, and sleep."

A hunk of dry bread, and a mouthful of cheese, washed down with snow, made their supper. Hungry, damp, cold, and thirsty beyond measure, Susan curled up between the roots of a tree. Her groundsheet was more of an affliction than a comfort. A long night of misery stretched ahead: sleep would never come. But come it did, and surprisingly quickly. A warm languor crept through her limbs: her brain told her to resist, but she could not. "This is how you freeze to death." "Well, there's nothing to be done about it now. And it's the . . . first . . . time I've been . . . warm . . . for years . . . years. . . ." The snow against her cheek was a pillow of swansdown. The scufflings of Gowther and Colin in their exhaustion and discomfort were carried far away beyond her reach. Susan slept.

It was a curious dream. Much of it seemed to be no more than a mixture of all her waking thoughts and wishes, timeless, disjointed, as difficult to hold as an image in rippling water. And then, for long periods, the people, and voices, and episodes of her dancing brain would fall into place, and become so vivid, so concrete, that there was nothing of dreaming about them. But always, after a while, the pattern would break. It was like a painting in which the brush strokes became detached from the canvas, and drifted away as isolated scraps of color, only to regroup themselves to show the scene advanced a little in time. But this was the main thread of Susan's dream.

She was sitting cross-legged with Colin, Gowther, and the dwarfs under the trees of the island. Before them were golden dishes piled high with meats, and spices, fruits, and cool, green cresses. Redesmere flashed blue in the light of high summer. Stromkarls were laughing and playing in the water, others listened to the music of the voice of Angharad Goldenhand. She sat between the children, dressed in a robe of white linen. She was tall, and slender, and fair; her long, plaited hair like red gold; and on her brow a band of gold.

It seemed that nothing of their adventures was unknown to her, and she had much to tell. The lios-alfar of the west, said Angharad, grew fewer every year. Only beyond

210

Minith Bannawg did they hold court in great numbers; and when they had heard rumor of the capture of Firefrost by Grimnir and the Morrigan, the elf-lord Atlendor son of Naf had come south to find what truth there was in the tale. He was ill of the smoke sickness when he reached the island, and Angharad nursed him to health. Then, when the stromkarl came from Goldenstone the previous evening, Atlendor decided to go back to his people, since news of Firefrost was good and there was need of him in Prydein. He had set out that morning, in haste to be clear of the sullied air, and he dared not stay for words when he put an end to the spies in Radnor wood.

The dream ran on in a world of sunlit laughter, and stromkarls brought Fenodyree and the children cloaks of red muspel hair, woven from the beards of giants, and lined with white satyrs' wool; and there were four cloaks sewn together to cover Gowther's broad shoulders.

"And for you," said Angharad Goldenhand, "for whom the danger is most real, take this bracelet of mine. It will guard you on your journey, and when the other is with Cadellin Silverbrow, think of this as fair exchange: it has many virtues."

She took from her arm a band of white metal, and fastened it about Susan's left wrist.

"May the Sleepers lie safe in Fundindelve."

"Thank . . . thank you."

Susan was overwhelmed a little by such generosity; normally it would have embarrassed her, but she could not be embarrassed in the warmth of Angharad's smile.

The picture dissolved once more, but those golden eyes, full of sunlight, remained steadfast through the wheeling colors of her dream.

"Thank you," said Susan.

The golden eyes faded.

"Thank you. Thank you!"

Her voice sounded loudly in her head; the kaleidoscope receded into a blank screen of consciousness, against which her words fell with a peculiar lack of resonance. Susan knew she was almost awake: awake to a world of snow, and hunger, and weariness, and great peril. Desperately she tried to force her way back into sleep, to make *that* reality, but the wall was too strong. One by one her senses returned. She felt air cutting into her lungs like blades of ice, and when a drifting snowflake landed gently on her cheek she groaned, and thrust her head into the crook of her elbow. Instantly Susan forced her eyes open, and strained to bring them into focus; but the remains of sleep were heavy upon her, and it was a full quarter of a minute before she knew beyond doubt that her cheek had not lied.

Susan was wrapped in a cloak of bronze-red hair, lined with a fleece of curls.

There was something enclosing her wrist, something that had not been there earlier. She worked her arm free of the cloak to see what it was. A silver bracelet.

The others were awake now. Colin and Gowther fingered their cloaks as though in a stupor. A waning moon shone in a clear sky of frost.

"But it was a *dream* . . . ! !"

212

". . . and the stromkarls. . . ."

"It conner have happened. . . ."

"Did you see . . . ?"

"So did I!"

"It was summer, too!"

". . . and all that food."

"Are you hungry?"

"No!"

"Theer's only our footprints in the snow, and all."

"But these cloaks. . . ."

"And what about this?" said Susan.

"Aye, that is a precious gift," said Durathror.

They had forgotten the dwarfs, in their astonishment.

"Oh, *hello!*" said Gowther. "I'm glad as somebody here knows what they're about! Witches, boggarts, and green freetings I've had to take in one day, and after that I conner feel inclined to argue with owt you say, but now that we're getting to the stage wheer I dunner know whether I'm sleeping or waking, I begin to wonder if I'm dreaming the whole lot!"

"Dreams, glamour, they are not easy to tell apart," said Fenodyree, "and men have ever thought dreams are not reality. The Lady of the Lake is a skilled weaver of enchantment. She knew that without help we could not have survived the night. Now, with muspel cloaks upon our backs, we need not fear the cold of fimbulwinter, even though the ice-giants themselves came south. And *that* gift may be more than all."

He pointed to the bracelet. It had an air of great age.

Along the outer face it was lightly incised, and inlaid with black enamel, much of which was missing. One half was a plain, coiling, leaf design, flanked by two oblongs of a diamond lattice pattern, with four spots within each diamond. On the other half, between two more oblongs, was an inscription in heavy, square lettering that was unknown to Susan.

"Yes, but in what way is it valuable?"

"I cannot tell you. But Angharad would not wear it for ornament alone."

"She might have told me what it was for, though."

"Perhaps it would not do for you to learn all its secrets at a time; sudden power is an evil, dangerous thing for any hands. Wear this always, guard it as you would the stone, and I know it will not fail you in need. And, above all, let it remind you of one who gave shelter and aid to those whose downfall would lift a weight of sorrow from her heart."

"What do you mean?" said Colin. "I don't understand. She's on our side, isn't she?"

"Aye, but you must know this: Angharad Goldenhand is wife to one who sleeps in Fundindelve; a great captain. A week had they been married when the king summoned his knights to go under the earth. Seven days of happiness to last her down the years. Do you see now how generous she has been? We are rescued, fed, and clothed, and are going on our way the better equipped for our task, yet, if we succeed, Angharad Goldenhand may not greet her lord for many a hundred years to come."

19

GABERLUNZIE

THE SUN had risen, but the mara were far beyond its reach as they reclined upon the floor under the lion's head in the Cave of the Svartmoot. Arthog and Slinkveal and other svarts were present, too, and there must have been fifty of the morthbrood ranged along its walls. In one corner what looked like a mound of rags, parchment-covered sticks, and old boots writhed and twitched. On top of the head stood Shape-shifter and Grimnir, and the cave was lit by the red glow of the firedrake held in the lap of the aged, piebald svart, in his seat below the lion's jaws. Selina Place was speaking in the Common Tongue.

". . . and a coven of our sisters killed by elves, and yet you saw nothing! Mossock and the children reach the far end of Radnor, yet *you* saw nothing! They *must* have passed you! Such incompetence, brother Galleytrot, could see us all in Ragnarok ere midnight."

"But they didn't pass me!" blustered James Henry Hodgkins. "I'd have seen them!"

"But they did, and you did not. One more error, dear brother, and you will be svart-meat.

"And while Ragnarok is on our lips, let us speak plainly to you all. Nastrond has no word of us, but he *will* hear, and when that time comes *all* your lives will be forfeit if we cannot wield the stone. Lest any of you have not our faith in success, you must know that the boundary is sealed. Any who try to cross will be slain: so let no one think to find favor with Nastrond through betrayal.

"Now to our plans. We do not believe the humans have survived the night. All dwellings and outhouses were watched, so they must have stayed in the open. Dwarfs are hardier, but we doubt if they can endure such cold, therefore we expect to hear news quickly. The search is to continue until the stone is found, for if it has passed to the elves all your efforts will be needed.

"Today the skies will be clear. This cannot be helped, since it will take till sunset to bring more cloud. By night we shall have enough to give unbroken cover for as long as we wish, though, so that you may follow tracks more easily, there will be no further snow. Thus the mara and the svart-alfar will be able to hunt throughout the day, if needs be.

"The lyblacs and the morthbrood will now go to relieve their fellows, and will pass on our instructions. Remember, the sky is full of eyes; cowards and traitors will not run far. That is all."

The heap of rags spilled over, and broke into a number of tattered forms, which rose jerkily to their feet like scarecrow marionettes, and slunk, spindly and stooping, out of the cave.

216

"It is not what you say Nastrond has learned from his spies that we fear, so much as his own mind," said Shape-shifter to Grimnir, closing the door of the broom cupboard after her. "We have felt it probing our thoughts often within the last month. There is no telling when he will act. And the svarts are not to be trusted if they fear us less: an example must be made of one or two without delay—that has always been the best encouragement. We shall have to 'unmask' a 'traitor' at the next moot."

With the first light, the island had grounded close to a stream on the opposite side of Redesmere from where the mara had lost the trail.

Clothed in the featureless snow, the countryside seemed vast; limitless as a desert, and as silent as a mine, the land offered no cover. Any movement against that background would be seen for miles, a line of footprints could not be missed, and in the brittle air any sound would carry undiminished to distant ears.

Durathror suggested, and the others reluctantly agreed, that their best course was to walk along the actual bed of the stream, but as close to the bank as possible. And so it was that, with the extra hardship of legs frozen from the knee down, they took up the pattern of the previous day's travel. Happily, the muspel cloaks had the property of sliding around obstacles without catching or tearing, and, worn with the lining on the outside, and the hood up, were good camouflage.

Ten minutes after sunrise, the first birds swept overhead. The morning wore on, monotonously, though not un-

217

eventfully. Half a dozen scarecrows were bypassed, and two pairs of hikers came near to achieving their purpose, and a swift death. But these moments, and an occasional set of footprints, were all that distracted attention from the task of wading upstream.

By noon they had advanced a little over a mile; then Gowther stopped.

"I've been thinking," he said. "If we follow this brook much longer we'll be turning north, and pushing up into Henbury, and we shanner be so very far from wheer we started. Now just over yonder is Pyethorne wood, and that borders on Thornycroft pools, and, if I remember, we'll find a stream as will take us in the reet direction from theer. Shall we have a look?"

Unfortunately, though, to gain the wood they had to skirt the edge of a field, cross a lane near to the lodge of Thornycroft hall, and make their way over two hundred and fifty yards of exposed parkland.

They managed to reach the lane undetected, but as they lay under the hedge, the remaining stages looked to be by far the worst check they had yet encountered.

"I see no way," said Durathror, creasing his eyes against the glare of the sunlit snow. "And to await night here would be madness."

"But do we have to go through there?" said Colin. "Can't we work round to somewhere else?"

"Aye, I've been thinking about yon, too," said Gowther, "but I doubt we shanner do better elsewheer. Sithee: if we go north we'll be moving back on Alderley, and we'll have put Macclesfield between us and wheer we want to get to. If we take our road round by the south, we'll have to pass through Gawsworth, unless we go quite a step out of our way; and if you'll be guided by me, we'll steer clear of Gawsworth, matters being as they are. Some mighty queer things happen theer at the best of times, without all this. No, Pyethorne wood's the place: it's our nearest water, and we should go no closer to Gawsworth than Dark Lane and Sugarwell, which is all to the good."

"I think we must choose your way," said Fenodyree after some argument. "But how are we to gain the wood?"

"We'll have to chance it," said Gowther. "And if we meet onybody, let's hope they know nowt about us. No, I hanner forgotten the birds, neither. But theer's been enough folks gone along this lane, and down the drive, for our tracks not to stond out a mile—especially if we watch wheer we tread. Now, if we flop down in a heap at the side of the drive every time the birds come over, and make sure as we've no bits and pieces sticking out from under our cloaks, we should be all reet. Now listen: you follow the drive till it binds reet almost at the hall. I'll go first, so as I con come back and tell you if theer's ony snags. Then you'll see two paths, one going left, and the other pretty near straight on to the wood. I just hope as how we shanner be the first to have used it today. Give me twenty minutes, and I'll meet you theer."

"Farmer Mossock," said Fenodyree, "I see we have a new

219

leader! Your shrewdness will take us to Shuttlingslow better than my slow wits!"

"No," said Gowther, "it's just that I like to be doing: so long!"

The sky was clear; he stepped into the road, and walked through the drive gateway, and past the lodge.

Twenty minutes later Susan and Durathror followed, and, ten minutes after, Colin and Fenodyree.

"The lodge was bad," said Susan, "but after the strain of that drive I nearly collapsed when we had to walk out in full view of the big house and all those staring windows."

"*We* had to drop flat twice in front of the house!" said Colin. "If anyone was watching, they must have thought we were mad."

"Aye, it was a bit strenuous, "said Gowther. "How do you think we fared?"

"The birds missed us, I think," said Fenodyree, "and I saw no one in the rooms. How was it with you, cousin?"

"I saw no one, and heard naught: we have done well."

But garrulous old Jim Trafford was a small man, and it was his afternoon off. By half past two he was in his accustomed corner in the Harrington Arms, and monopolizing the conversation of four of his acquaintances.

"I reckon it's twice as cowd as it were eleven year back," he said. "I've seen nowt like it; it's enough fer t'send you mazed. Eh, and I think it's takken one or two like that round 'ere this morning. No, listen! It were nobbut a couple of hours since, nawther. I were up at th'all, going round seeing as they was orreet fer coal afore I come away, and one o' th'fires were low, like, so I gets down fer t'give it a poke. Well, I'm straightening up again, and I 'appens fer t'look out o' th'winder, and what does I see? I'll tell yer. Theer was two little fellers, about so 'igh, gooing past th' 'ouse towards Pyethorne. No, listen! They wore white capes, wi' 'oods as come over their faces, and they kept peering round, and up, and down, and walking 'alf back'ards. I'll swear as one 'em 'ad a beard—a yeller un it were. It's th' gospel truth!

"Well, I shakes me 'ead, and carries me bucket into th' next room. Fire's orreet theer, but scuttle wants a lump or two. On me way out I looks through th' winder, and theer they are again! And this time I sees a good bit o' beard, but now it's black!

"Round and round they scowls, then they drops flat on their faces, and pull their 'eads and legs in like tortoises. It's a fact! You conner 'ardly see 'em agen th' snow. Well, after a minute or two, they gets up, and off they trots, back to back now, if you please! Then smack on their faces again! I tell yer, I couldner 'ardly credit it. I watches them while they're near to th' wood, then they puts down their 'eads, and runs! It's this 'ere frost what's be'ind it, and no error. Theer'll be a few like them, I'll tell thee, if we 'ave much more o' this. . . . Eh, Fred! What's to do? Art feeling ill? What's th' 'urry?"

The door slammed.

"Eh, what's up wi' 'im? Eh, you lot, come over 'ere! See at Fred! 'E's gooing up th' avenue as though 'is breeches was on fire!

"I tell yer, it's the weather!"

Pythorne wood is not large. Much of it is little more than a neck of land dividing the two lakes of Thorneycroft hall, and it was in this part of the wood that Gowther waited for the others to join him. Together again, they decided to rest for an hour or so before exploring the far end of the lake to the east of the hall.

"We must keep guard by turns," said Fenodyree. "Durathror and I shall divide the night between us, and, until we reach the forest, one of you will watch over the midday halt. Is it agreed?"

They curled up in their muspel cloaks, and forgot the snow. Even their ice-bound feet grew warm, and after such a morning, sleep was not long in coming.

Colin had offered to take the first turn. He sat upon a tree stump, and looked about him, seeing the beauty of the day for the first time. The air was still; and although the sun shone in a cloudless sky, there was not enough warmth in its rays to melt the thin blades of snow that stood inches high even to the tips of the slenderest twigs on every tree. Pyethorne was a wood of lace that day. There had been floes on Redesmere at dawn, but now the ice here was unbroken, thick, and blue as steel.

Out across the ice was an island, so overgrown with trees

222

that it was as though they sprouted straight out of the lake; and at first that was all Colin could see; but as the minutes went by something began to take shape within the trees. The impression was strongest when he did not look directly at the island, but, even so, for long enough he could not be certain that there *was* anything there. And then, like a hidden figure in a picture puzzle, it came unexpectedly into focus, and Colin gasped. It was a square tower, old, ruinous, so hemmed in by trees that if Colin had had anything other to do than sit and look about him for an hour and a half, he would never have noticed it.

I must see how long it takes the others to find that, he thought, laughing at his own blindness, and he continued his watch.

Then, oddly, the tower began to grow on Colin's nerves. He felt that it was staring at him with its expressionless eyes. He sat with his back to it, but that made matters worse, and he had to turn around. Imagination, he told himself. A tower could not help but look sinister in that condition; obviously no one lived there. But Colin could not settle unless he was facing the tower.

He began to range his eyes from left to right, across the lake and back again, but never once did he look directly at the island. And, of course, the urge to do so grew stronger. Worse, he thought how unpleasant it would be if he turned his head, and saw—something. Then, in his imagination, he pictured these "somethings," and from that it was a simple step to believing they really were there.

223

Colin drew a deep breath. Having allowed himself to be worked into such a state, there was only one thing to do. He looked full at the tower.

His yelp of fright brought the dwarfs bounding to their feet. There, not forty yards away, among the outer trees of the island, was a man dressed all in black, and seated on a black horse, and his eyes were fixed on Colin.

"What is wrong?" whispered Fenodyree, but Colin could only point. At this the rider began to walk his horse toward them across the ice. In silence they watched him come.

He was tall, and sparely built, though little of him could be seen under his full cloak. Black riding boots, silver spurred, came to his knees; on his head was a wide-brimmed hat. His hair, green as a raven's wing, curled on his shoulders, framing a lean, brown face. Small gold rings pierced his ears; and his eyes were blue—a fierce blue, burning with an intensity to rival the heart of Firefrost.

When he was still some yards away he reined in his horse.

"I have been looking for you," he said in a deep voice. Yet it was not only deep, but soft also, with a lilt in it that was not Scots, or Irish, or Welsh, but could have been all three. Some of the apprehension that had been gripping Gowther and the children left them.

"Welcome, Gaberlunzie," said Fenodyree. "Yesterday we saw you from afar, but could not be sure. Will you not come among the trees? The Morrigan and her brood harry us, and the spies are out."

224

The stranger looked at the sky.

"I thought there were no birds," he said.

He dismounted, and brought his horse under the trees. Fenodyree quickly told their story, and the man called Gaberlunzie heard him in silence.

"And therefore we must be on Shuttlingslow at Friday's dawn to meet Cadellin Silverbrow, or the world we know may not endure. Will you stay with us, and help us?"

The blue eyes stared into space; then Gaberlunzie gave his answer.

"I shall not bide. Listen to my say. Beyond Minith Bannawg there is trouble breeding greater than this—or so we fear. The lios-alfar of the north are not enough to act alone. So I have come to gather to their aid kinsmen and allies. I have wandered through Dyfed's plundered land, along the shores of Talebolion, many a weary month to Sinadon. And I am needed in Prydein within the week.

"I stopped by Fundindelve to ask for help but there was no answer, only the morthbrood. The storm caught me before I could reach Angharad Goldenhand, and when darkness came I heard the mara and sought this island without delay. It was a cold swim, and the sun rose before I dared to sleep.

"I must turn northwards this day: my duty lies there. But what help there is in me you shall have before I go. If I leave you at the forest by nightfall, will that serve you well?"

"That would almost end our labors," said Fenodyree.

225

"But, alas, we dare not move openly: by day the skies are watchful, and by night the mara walk. We crawl on our bellies to our noble end!"

"But now you will ride!" laughed Gaberlunzie. "No, I do not trifle with you."

"*Look! !*" cried Susan, her voice hoarse with alarm.

So intent had they been that they had not noticed the wall of mist come creeping over the snow. Like a white smoke it curled among the trees, and eclipsed the far end of the lake even as Susan spoke.

"Grimnir!" said Durathror.

"Whist now!" said Gaberlunzie, who was the only one undisturbed. "Sit you all down again. It is nothing of the sort. It is what I have been expecting. Cloudless skies, snow, such frost as this, and darkness not two hours away —what more natural than a good, white mist to blind the morthbrood and speed us on our road? Now onto my horse, and away!"

The fog was about them, absolute.

"You hold on a minute!" said Gowther. "Before we try to fit six on one horse, I'd like to know how you think we're going to find our way in this lot. It's about as much as I can do to see my feet."

"Do not worry, friend: my eyes are not your eyes, and my horse is not of earthly stock: we shall not stumble. But come! Are we to argue here until the day of doom? Mount!"

226

And they did mount. Durathror and Fenodyree bunched together in front of Gaberlunzie; behind him sat the children, and behind *them* Gowther, his arms on either side of Colin and Susan, holding Gaberlunzie's cloak in his fists.

Gowther expected to come off within a minute of starting—that is, if the horse *could* start. But a flick of the rein and they were away like the wind; no horse ever sped so smoothly. Fields, hedges, ditches, flowed under its hoofs. The snow muffled all noise of their passage as they plunged full tilt through the mist. The air whipped about them, and their hands grew black, and cold grasped their heads as if with pincers.

After a while they left hedges behind, the land became broken and uneven, but they did not falter. Wide trenches opened under them, one after another, dangerously deep; and ghostly, broken walls, gaping like the ruins of an ancient citadel, lowered on either side. It was as though they were riding out of their own time back to a barbaric age, yet they were running only by the peat stacks of Danes Moss, a great tract of bogland that lay at the foot of the hills.

Trench after trench they crossed, and each a check to the morthbrood, should they follow after; for Gaberlunzie was of a cunning race. And so they came into the hills, and down to a lonely road in a valley.

"We are in the forest now," said Gaberlunzie.

He swung his horse off the road, and in one sailing leap

they were among the trees. A broad path cut upwards through the close-set ranks, and here Gaberlunzie slowed to a walk.

"I shall not stop; you must leave as best you may, so that my trail will be unbroken. Do not stop to cover your own, but look for a place of shelter. Later you will see foxes: do not harm them."

"But what of yourself?" said Fenodyree. "It will not do to be abroad after sunset."

"The morthbrood are welcome to the chase! For I shall go by Shining Tor, and Cat's Tor, and Windgather Rocks, and the sun will rise for me out of the three peaks of Eildon. I do not think the morthbrood will be then so keen."

Five minutes later they said their good-byes, and tumbled into the snow.

"Do as I have said," called Gaberlunzie, "and you will come to no harm here; and when you meet Cadellin, say I wish him well."

Durathror was the last to leave, and as he picked himself up, the form of Gaberlunzie, one hand raised in farewell, blended into the mist, and passed out of his sight forever.

"I don't like the idea of leaving all these tracks," said Colin.

"There is little else we can do," said Fenodyree. "And I feel that Gaberlunzie knows what he is about. Our task is to hide, and this is the place. Take care lest you shake the snow from the branches!"

The trees grew only a few feet apart, and the sweeping

228

branches came close to the ground, so close that even the dwarfs had to crawl, while Gowther had to pull himself along on his stomach.

They went downhill from the path a good way before Fenodyree stopped.

"Here will be as safe as anywhere. Even without the mist you can see no more than a few yards. Let us make ourselves as comfortable as we can, for we shall not stir again until we go to greet Cadellin."

Down the path through the forest two slim shadows moved. Coming to the trampled snow, and the trail leading under the branches, they stopped, and sniffed. And then they began to roll and frolic all around; two foxes sporting on a winter hillside. When every trace of human feet was obliterated, they set off down the trail, throwing the snow into confusion as they fought.

The sound of their approach reached the dwarfs' ears, and they waited, sword in hand, for whatever was drawing near. Then the foxes tumbled into sight, and landed on their haunches, side by side, flecked with snow, their red tongues lolling, and their sharp eyes narrowing, in a wicked, panting grin.

For a while they sat there, and Durathror was about to speak, but they flung up their tails, and streaked away downhill.

"Thank you," said Fenodyree.

"Why?" said Colin. "What were they doing?"

"Covering our tracks rather well, I reckon," said Gowther. "Now yon's what I *call* clever."

"And the scent of a fox is stronger than that of either men or dwarfs," said Durathror, smiling.

He smiled again, alone to himself in the night while the others slept, when he heard the baying of hounds pass over the hill, and fade into the far distance.

20

SHUTTLINGSLOW

No one slept much all through the second, and last, night in the forest. It had been a strain on the nerves to lie inactive, yet constantly alert, for a whole day. The cold was no longer a problem, and the food of Angharad was safeguard against hunger and thirst for many days, so there had been nothing to do but wait, and think.

It was as though the night would never end: yet they could find little to talk about, wrapped in their cloaks, five dim shapes against the lighter background of the snow.

And, because of the snow, it was never quite dark, even in the forest: and although they could not approach the dwarfs' powers of sight the children found that, as the night wore on, they could see well enough to distinguish between individual trees and the hillside.

Tension mounted with every hour. But at last Fenodyree said:

"Dawn is not far off. Are we ready?"

They climbed up the path. The marks of hoofs were still

there for the dwarfs to see, but they were overlaid with many tracks; hound, svart, and others.

After a long drag uphill they came above the forest onto a bleak shelf of moorland; and out of the far side of the plateau, half a mile distant, the last two hundred feet of Shuttlingslow reared black against the paling night.

They halted, and stared, prey to their emotions at the sudden appearance of the long-sought goal. It was so very near.

"Yonder it is," said Durathror, "but shall we ever reach it?"

They looked cautiously around. The snow lay two feet deep upon the moor. Not a tree could be seen in the gloom; only a dark line of wall, the dry stone walling of the hills, cut across the landscape. Once committed to this waste, once they had made their mark, there could be no drawing back. And after all those miles of stealth it seemed madness to walk out across such naked land. More, an actual fear of the open spaces came over them, even the dwarfs; they felt light-headed, and weak-kneed, and longed for the security of a close horizon.

Then Gowther squared his shoulders. "Come on," he said, "let's be doing." And he strode off toward Shuttlingslow.

It was a hard trek, and a stiff climb at the end of it, but both were achieved without sight of the morthbrood or any of their kind. Up they toiled, hands and feet working

232

together on the near-perpendicular slope; up and up, till their lungs felt torn and their hearts were bursting. Thirty feet more! They had done it! In spite of all the forces ranged against them, they had done it!

They lay panting on the flat summit ridge. All about them was nothing but the air. When exultation had died, they crawled around until they were lying in a rough horseshoe, facing outwards. In this way, while keeping together, they could watch all the surrounding land except for the southern approach, which was hidden by the far end of the ridge. The crest of Shuttlingslow is only a few yards wide, and they were able to talk without raising their voices.

Fenodyree reckoned that dawn was less than half an hour away. All eyes strained to pick out Cadellin as soon as he should appear. Once Durathror thought he saw him, but it was a troll-woman striding across a hillside miles away. It grew lighter. North, south, and east, the hills rolled away, and to the west, the plain, a lake of shadow into which the night was sinking.

"Isn't it time we were seeing him?" Colin asked. He could now see the straight track they had drawn across the plateau. The others too, were glancing in that direction.

"The sun has not yet risen," said Fenodyree. "He will come."

But he did not come. And soon they could no longer pretend that it was night. There was no break in the ceiling of cloud, but the day would not be denied.

"It looks as if we've shot our bolt, dunner it?" said Gowther. "Do we just lie here and wait to be picked like ripe apples?"

"We must wait until the last moment," said Fenodyree. "And wherever we go now we shall not escape the eyes of the morthbrood."

"It looks like being a grand day, then; Friday the thirteenth and all!"

"Aye," said Durathror. " 'Between nine and thirteen all sorrow shall be done.' "

Their spirits drained from them: their trail stood out as clearly as if it had been painted black. And there was no Cadellin.

Occasional specks moved singly or in groups across the white backdrop of hills, and out on the plain, from the smudge that was Alderley Edge, drifted what might have been a plume of smoke, but was not.

"Now that they are astir," said Durathror, "Cadellin must needs come quickly, or he will come too late."

As it gained height the column of birds split into patrolling flocks, two of which headed toward Shuttlingslow. When they were a mile away it became obvious that one flock would pass to the south of the hill, and the other to the north. The northerly flock raced over the plateau, and the watchers on the hilltop wanted to close their eyes. Suspense did not last. The leader swung around in a tight circle over the line of footprints, and brought the flock slowly along the trail, close to the ground.

234

"*Do not move!*" whispered Fenodyree. "It is our only chance."

But the muspel cloaks were not proof against keen eyes at close range. The whole flock shot skywards on the instant, and broke north, south, east, and west to din the alarm. One or two remained, at a safe height, and they cruised in beady silence. The specks in the distance slowed, changed course, and began to move in toward a common center—Shuttlingslow. More appeared, and more still, and distant, thin voices were raised in answer to the summons, and mingled with them the whine of the mara, and a baying note, that the children had heard once before at St. Mary's Clyffe, and Fenodyree more recently in the forest. From all over the plain clouds of birds were rushing eastwards. Durathror stood up.

"Is this the end of things, cousin?"

"It may be."

"Where is Cadellin Silverbrow?"

"I cannot think; unless it be that he is dead, or prisoner, and either way *we* are lost."

"But if he's coming from *that* direction," cried Colin, pointing south, "we shouldn't see him until he was right at the top!"

"Fool that I am! Quick! We may throw away all hope by standing here!"

Halfway along the ridge the birds attacked. In a cloud they fell, clawing and pecking, and buffeting with their wings. And their attentions were directed against Susan above all. In the first seconds of advantage they fastened upon her like leeches, and tangled thickly in her hair. And their strength was human. But before they could drag her from the hill Dyrnwyn and Widowmaker were among them.

Backwards and forwards along the crest the conflict raged, until the ground was red and black, and still they came. Not before fully a quarter of their number had been hewn from the air did they abandon the fight.

Durathror and Fenodyree leaned on their swords, heads hanging. All were torn and bleeding; but the wounds were not deep.

"It is well they broke," panted Fenodyree, "for I was near spent."

"Aye," said Durathror, "it will go hard with us if they come again."

Gowther reversed his grip on his ash stick, which he had been wielding with terrible effect, and pointed.

"And yon have not been idle, sithee. We'll have to be thinking quick!"

The morthbrood were pouring in from all sides; only to the southwest was the land not thickly dotted with running figures. The near groups were not heading for the top of Shuttlingslow, but were moving to encircle it; and out of the valley of Wildboarclough, seven hundred feet below at the foot of the hill's eastern slope, came a band of svarts, five hundred strong. There was no Cadellin.

"Can we stem this flood, cousin?" said Fenodyree.

Durathror shook his head.

236

"By weight of numbers they will conquer. But since it has come to this we must draw what teeth we may before we go down to rest. And it is how I would wish to die, for so have I lived."

"Well, *I'm* not going to let them have the stone as easily as that!" cried Susan. "You stay if you like, but I'm off!"

And she started down the hill at a mad speed toward where the numbers of the morthbrood were thinnest.

"Come back, Sue!" shouted Colin.

"No!" said Gowther. "She's the only one round here as is talking sense. Well, come on! Are you fain to let her go by herself?"

They sprang after Susan; floundering in the snow, leaping, bounding, falling, rolling, they hurtled after her, unmindful of bruises, caring nothing for safety, while the air clamored with the shriek of birds.

Once off the escarpment their gait slackened, yet they were making every effort to hurry. The snow was knee-deep, and clogged the feet like a nightmare. Rocks, reed clumps, hummocks of grass sent them stumbling at every stride. The birds flew low but did not attack.

Over Piggford moor Susan ran, flanked by dwarfs with gleaming swords. A few stray svarts, and the loose-limbed scarecrow creatures barred the way from time to time, but they fell back at the sight of the hard blades. They preferred to join the crowd that was now sweeping around the sides of Shuttlingslow.

The moor curved down three hundred feet to a stream

237

that Susan did not discover in time, and they all slithered into the water, and lost precious seconds there. Choking, they scrambled up the opposite hill. And that climb exhausted the last of their strength. It beat them mentally as well as physically, for it was a convex slope, and the skyline, the apparent top of the hill, was always receding. It was never far away, but they could never reach it. Soon it was nearly beyond them to climb the stone walls that blocked their path, and when they did totter to the crest, and saw that it was only a wide shelf, and that a further incline awaited them, all but Durathror collapsed as though their legs had been cut from under them.

Durathror looked behind him. Except for one or two stragglers, Piggford moor was bare. Yet the noise of the chase was loud: he heard it clearly, even through the bedlam of the milling birds. The morthbrood must have crossed the stream.

"*Up!*" he cried. But they were not at the top of the final rise when the pursuit came into sight. The svarts, with their snow-skimming feet, and the tireless, bobbing lyblacs had outstripped the morthbrood, and they had at their head one that was worse than all—a mara, gray and terrible. And before the mara ran the two hounds of the Morrigan, their blind heads low to the scent, and their mouths hanging red.

"Stay not for me!" shouted Durathror, facing about.

For a second Fenodyree wavered, then he nodded, and pushed the others on toward the crest of the hill.

The hounds were well ahead of the mara, and the first, drawing near, slowed to a walk, ears pricked forward.

"Ha!" cried Durathror.

The hound paused.

"Ha!"

And as it leaped he ducked, and thrust upwards with both hands to his sword, and the beast was dead before it hit the ground. But it wrenched Dyrnwyn from Durathror's grasp in its fall, and then the other sprang. But Durathror was lightning itself in battle, and the teeth closed not on his throat, but on his forearm which he rammed between the wet jaws, and over he went, hurled onto his back by the weight of the monster. And while they wrestled the mara strode by unheedingly.

Durathror fumbled for the dagger at his waist: he found it, and the end was quick.

But he could do nothing to save the others. Already the mara towered over them. Bravely, rashly, Fenodyree launched himself upon it, but Widowmaker flew from his hands in a shower of sparks at the first blow, and, leaning down from its twenty feet of grim might, the troll grasped Susan by the wrist, and plucked her from the ground.

The scream that cut the air then stopped svarts and lyblacs in their tracks, and even the birds were hushed. Durathror hid his face, and groaned; tears flooded his cheeks. Again the piteous cry, but weaker now. Durathror knew his heart must break. Again. And again. Shouting wildly,

239

mad with grief, he rose, and snatched for his sword. But the sight that met him brought him straight to his knees. For, limp, in the snow, just as she had fallen, was Susan. Beside her was the mara, *and it was shrinking!* Like a statue of butter in a furnace heat it writhed and wasted. Its contours melted into formlessness as it dwindled. No sound did it utter again, save a drawn-out moan as movement finally ceased. And there on the moor-top stood a rough lump of rock.

Half-unconscious, Susan knew little of the mara's fate. As the spiral-patterned clouds and flashing lights withdrew from before her eyes she could only stare at Angharad's bracelet, dented and misshapen from the grip of the stone-cold hand that had fastened upon her wrist.

"Are you all reet, lass?"

"What did you *do?*"

"I'm not hurt. It was the bracelet, I think. What's happened?"

The svarts and the lyblacs were in confusion, and, for the moment, lacked the united courage to advance. Durathror was quick to seize the chance. He faced the crowd, and spoke in a voice for all to hear.

"See how the invincible perish! If such is the fate of the mara, how shall *you* endure our wrath? Let him who loves not life seek to follow further!"

The mob slunk back. But now the morthbrood were at hand, and they were not to be so promptly awed. He knew he had won only a breathing space—just long enough to prevent their being overrun while Susan gathered her strength.

And then Durathror saw what he had lost all hope of seeing: a lone man on the top of Shuttlingslow, two miles away. And as he looked he saw the tall figure leave the crest, and begin to descend.

Durathror joined the others; they, too, had seen.

"But I dunner think yon bunch have," said Gowther. "Now how are we going to hold out while he gets here?"

"It is an hour's journey over this ground," said Fenodyree.

The morthbrood were conferring with the svarts: there was much shouting, and waving of hands. The svarts were not keen to risk the mara's end, while the morthbrood did not want to take the brunt of the dwarfs' swordsmanship themselves. The Morrigan, in her black robes, was screaming furiously.

"Cowards! Liars! They are but *five!* Take them! Take them *now!*"

Fenodyree did not wait for more.

"Come," he said. "We cannot hold them if *she* is here. We must seek where we may make a stand against them."

A hundred yards was all they had, and as soon as they moved, the morthbrood surged after them. From the beginning there was little promise of escape, but when they crossed over the top of the hill, and came to a deeply sunk, walled lane, and saw warlocks streaming along it from both sides, they realized finally that this was the end of all pursuits, and, though it may seem strange, they were glad. The long struggle was nearly over, either way: a load of responsibility was lifted from their hearts.

"We shall run while we can!" cried Fenodyree; and he jumped down into the lane and pulled himself over the wall on the other side. "Look for a place for swords!"

But they had no choice. Lyblacs, armed with staves, thronged the side of the valley below them.

"A circle!" shouted Gowther. "Colin! Susan! Into th' middle!"

And so they took their stand: and all evil closed upon them.

"They are not to die, yet!" cried the Morrigan. "Who takes a life shall answer with his own!"

Back to back the dwarfs and Gowther fought, silently, and desperately. And in between crouched the children. The bestial shouts, the grunts and squeals of dying svarts, echoed from valley to valley. Fenodyree and Durathror wove a net of light with their swords as they slashed, and parried, and thrust. And when Gowther swung his stick skulls split and bones cracked. Their one hope was to survive until the wizard came; but where an enemy fell there was always another to take his place; and another, and another, and another, and another.

They fought themselves to a standstill. Gowther's stick was knocked from his hands, but he bent and took up a svart-hammer in either hand, and from that moment the slaughter increased. Following his example, the weaponless children snatched themselves weapons, and entered into the fight.

And thus for a while the battle ran their way. But it was the last flare of a guttering candle before the night swamps all. The end came suddenly. A svart-hammer crashed home above Fenodyree's elbow, and the bone snapped with the noise of a whiplash. His sword arm hanging useless, Fenodyree was a broken wall, and soon the enemy would pour through the breach. Durathror acted. He pushed out his free hand behind him while keeping his eyes fixed on his work.

"The stone! Give me the stone!"

Without questioning, Susan ducked behind Gowther, took off the chain bracelet, and locked it about Durathror's wrist. As she did so, a dozen pairs of hands clutched her, and dragged her backwards: but too late. Durathror sprang into the air. Valham enfolded him, and he turned toward Shuttlingslow in a last attempt to save the stone.

And the birds fell upon him like black hail. He disappeared from sight as though into a thundercloud. The lightning of his sword flashed through the smoke of birds, and the earth grew dark with their bodies: but there were also white eagle feathers, with blood upon them, and their number grew.

The battle on the ground was done: all eyes were upon that in the air. Nothing of Durathror could be seen as the cloud moved slowly away, but few birds were dropping now.

243

Lower down the hillside a round knoll stood out from the slope, topped by a thin beech wood; and on its crown a tall pillar of gritstone jutted to the sky like a pointing finger. Clulow was its name.

Over this mound the last blow was struck. A white object fluttered out of the base of the mass, hovered for a moment, pitched forward, and crashed through the trees, and lay still.

Down rushed the lyblacs and the svarts, howling. At the noise, the figure stirred. Durathror raised his head. Then he hauled himself upright against a gray trunk, steadied himself, and began to walk up the hill. He lurched and stumbled from tree to tree. His mail shirt was ripped half from his back, and Valham hung in ribbons. Often he would stand, swaying on his feet, and it seemed that he must fall backwards, but always he would stagger on, bent almost double, more wound than dwarf, and, at the last, leaning his full weight upon his sword.

So Durathror came to the pillar of stone. He put his back against it, and unclasped his belt. Loosening it, he threw it around the column, and buckled it tightly under his arms so that he should not fall. When this was done, he grasped Dyrnwyn in both hands, and waited.

For ten yards around, the hilltop was bare of trees, and at the edge of the circle the svarts halted, none wanting to be the first to cross the open ground and meet that sword. But it was only for a moment.

"There is the stone!" cried Shape-shifter from behind. "*Take it!*"

"Gondemar!" thundered Durathror.

Where he found the strength is a mystery and a great wonder. But such was his fury that none could withstand him, not even Arthog, lord of the svart-alfar, that was as big as a man. In the thick of the press he came against Durathror, and Durathror brought his sword around in an arc. The svart parried with his hammer, but Dyrnwyn clove through the stone, and Arthog's head leaped from his shoulders. But no sword can shear through stone unpunished, and at the next stroke the blade snapped halfway to the hilt. Yet still Durathror fought, and none who faced him drew breath again; and the time came when the svarts and lyblacs fell back to the trees to regain their strength and to prepare a last assault.

Durathror sagged in his harness, and the stump of Dyrnwyn hung by his side. His head dropped forward onto his chest, and a silence lay upon the hill.

21

THE HEADLESS CROSS

GRIMNIR RAN. Fear, excitement, greed drove him.

From the top of Shuttlingslow he had watched the chase right to the fall of the mara; and from that high vantage point he had seen something else, something approaching rapidly, away to the north, and although he had been on his guard against danger from that quarter for months, the form it had taken, and the time it had chosen to appear, could not have disturbed him more.

He came unnoticed over the hill above Clulow soon after Arthog died, when every eye was upon Durathror as the svarts withdrew from that still figure with the splintered sword. His gaze rested on the prisoners, each held by two warlocks of the morthbrood, standing between the main body and the wood; and Grimnir checked his stride, hope and distrust conflicting within him.

For above the clearing in the wood circled a carrion crow. It spiraled down, barely moving its wings, and came to rest on top of the standing-stone. A long time it perched there, watching, motionless. The silence was overpowering.

246

And then the crow launched itself into the air, and resumed its measured glide. Closer to the drooping warrior it came, closer . . . closer, *and settled on his shoulder*. But Durathror did not move. His trial was over.

A sigh rose through the trees, and the crow hopped from the dwarf's shoulder to the ground. Straight to his wrist it went: and from there back to the pillar, with Firefrost dangling at its beak. The bird threw up its head, neck feathers blown into a ruff, and, with wings outstretched, began to dance a clumsy jig. It rolled grotesquely from side to side, its head bobbing up and down, and a yell of triumph burst forth on every side.

Grimnir cast a quick glance over his shoulder. Yes, he must act at once. If the crow should drop its eyes and look above the throng it could not fail to notice . . . Swiftly he strode down the hill and pushed through the morthbrood. And as he went a new cry moved with him; for in turning to see who was coming so impetuously from behind, the crowd looked beyond him . . . and panicked.

Colin, Susan, Gowther, and Fenodyree had watched Durathror's battle in an agony of helplessness. Fury and despair had done their worst; their minds were numb with shock. So it was with little interest or emotion that they turned their heads when the note of fear ran through the morthbrood. Then Grimnir came upon them. He faltered, but only for a second. "Kill them," he said to the guards.

247

Susan opened her mouth, but no sound would come. For the first time in memory or legend Grimnir had spoken. And the voice was the voice of Cadellin.

The morthbrood were scattering in all directions. The guards were more intent on saving their own lives than on taking life away from others. For this is what they saw. Racing out of the north was a cloud, lower than any that hid the sun, and black. Monstrous it was, and in shape a ravening wolf. Its loins fell below the horizon, and its lean body arched across the sky to pouncing shoulders, and a head with jaws agape that even now was over the far end of the valley. Eyes glowed yellow with lightning, and the first snarls of thunder were heard above the cries of the morthbrood. There seemed to be one thought in all their minds—escape. But when Managarm of Ragnarok is about his master's bidding, such thoughts are less than dreams.

The svarts and lyblacs were beginning to break when Grimnir entered the wood. He kicked and trampled through them toward the pillar. The crow was still there, squatting low, its head deep in its shoulders, glaring at the oncoming cloud. It saw Grimnir on the edge of the clearing, read his purpose in a flash, and sprang. But Grimnir was too agile. He jumped, snatched high, and his fingers closed about the bird's scaly shins, and swept it out of the air. The other thin, gloved hand wrenched Firefrost from its beak. Grimnir cast the heap of feathers viciously against the pillar, and fled.

"Eh up!" said Gowther. "Here he comes again!"

The children and Fenodyree were still groping at the implications of what had just happened and it was not until Gowther cried, "And he's getten thy bracelet!" that they came back to life.

They might not have been there for the notice the morthbrood and all the rest took of them. Even Grimnir ignored them as he sped up toward the lane.

"After him!" shouted Fenodyree. "He must not escape!"

The hillside was thick with pell-mell bodies, but Grimnir could not be easily lost, and they set off blindly, without thinking what they could do if they caught him. Grimnir leaped onto the wall and stood poised, as though staring at something in the lane. Then he turned, and ran back down the hill, moving faster than ever. But Grimnir had barely left the wall when he staggered, and a sharp cry broke from him, and he toppled onto his hands. A double-edged sword stood out from his back. Along the blade coiled two serpents of gold, and so bright were they that it pained the eyes to look on them.

Slowly Grimnir rose, until he was on his feet. The sword dropped to the ground. He took three steps, swayed, and fell backwards. The deep cowl slid from his face, and the madness was complete. It was the face of Cadellin, twisted with pain, but nevertheless Cadellin; kind, noble, wise, his silver beard tucked inside the rank, green, marsh-smelling, monk-like habit of Grimnir the hooded one.

Susan thought she was out of her mind. Colin could not think or speak. Fenodyree wept. Then there was a crunching of rock above them, and they looked up: some-one was climbing over the wall. It was Cadellin.

He came toward them over the snow, and his eyes too, were full of tears. No words were spoken in greeting, for it was a moment beyond words. Cadellin dropped on one knee beside Grimnir, and the tears spilled onto his cheeks.

"Oh, Govannon!" he whispered. "Govannon!"

Grimnir opened his eyes.

"Oh, my brother! This is the peak of the sorrow of all my years. That it should come to this! And at my hand!"

Grimnir raised himself on one elbow, and, ignoring Cadellin, twisted his head toward the wood. An eager light gleamed in his eyes. Among all the haphazard scuttling, one figure moved with a set purpose, and that was Selina Place, who was running toward the little group as fast as she could, her robes streaming behind her.

Grimnir brought his head around, and stared at his brother, but he did not speak. Their eyes spoke through the barrier of years, and across the gulf of their lives.

Again Grimnir turned to Selina Place. She was close. He looked up into the smoking jaws of Managarm, then at Cadellin. A bleak smile touched the corners of his mouth, and he lifted his fist, and dropped the stone into Cadellin's hand, and fell back, dead.

Cadellin took up the sword, and sheathed it. He strove to keep his voice level.

"I am sorry we could not meet at dawn," he said. "I did not expect to come upon the mara." He looked at Fire-

250

frost resting in his palm. "Nor did I expect this. There will be much to tell in Fundindelve. But first . . ."

He turned to the Morrigan. She stood a dozen yards away, glowering, uncertain. She was not sure what had happened. Then Cadellin held up Firefrost for her to see.

"Get you to Ragnarok!"

Selina Place, fury in every line of her, shrieked and ran. And as she ran a change came over her. She seemed to bend low over the ground, and she grew smaller; her robes billowed out at her side; her thin legs were thinner, her squat body heavier; and then there was no Selina Place, only a carrion crow rising into a sky of jet.

"Make haste," said Cadellin, "or we ourselves shall be lost. Gowther Mossock, will you stand here in front of me? I shall put my hand on your shoulder. Colin, Susan, stand on either side: take hold of my robe: do not let go. Fenodyree, sit by our feet: cling fast to my hem. Is Durathror not with you?"

"He is here," said Fenodyree. "But he will not come again."

"What is it you say?"

Fenodyree pointed.

"Durathror! Quick! We must guard him!"

"Stay!" cried Fenodyree as Cadellin made toward the wood. "There is not time, and it would be of no use. See! Managarm is on us!"

All the sky to the north and east was wolf head. The mouth yawned wider, till there was nothing to be seen but the black, cavernous maw, rushing down to swallow hill and valley hole. Witches, warlocks, svarts, lyblacs, stampeded southwards, crushing underfoot any that blocked the way. The birds outdistanced them all, but they were not swift enough.

One bird alone did not go south. It flew toward the advancing shadow, climbing ever higher, until it was a black dot against a blacker vault, and even a dwarf's eyes could not tell if it did clear the ragged fangs that sought to tear it from the sky.

As the hill slid down the boundless throat Cadellin lifted his right hand, and held Firefrost on high. Gowther stood firm. Colin and Susan clasped their arms about Cadellin's waist, and Fenodyree grappled to him with his one good arm as much of the wizard's robes as he could hold.

"Drochs, Muroch, Esenaroth!"

A cone of light poured down from the stone, enclosing them in a blue haze. A starving wind, howling like wolves, was about them, yet the air they breathed was still. Slanting yellow eyes were seen dimly through the veil; hungry eyes. And there were other noises and other shapes that were better left unknown.

The fury raged and beat against the subtle armor, but it was as nothing to the power of Cadellin Silverbrow with Firefrost in his hand.

And at last, at once, the darkness passed, and the blue light faded. Blinking in the sunlight of a brilliant sky, the survivors of the wrath of Nastrond looked out over

252

fields of white; wind-smoothed, and as empty of life as a polar shore. No svart or lyblac stained the snow; no gaunt figure lay close by; the pillar of Clulow was bare. Away to the south a black cloud rolled. There was joy, and many tears.

And this tale is called the Weirdstone of Brisingamen. And here is an end of it.

3